Rupert Smith was born in Washington DC and grew up in Surrey. He is the author of two previous novels – *I Must Confess* and *Fly on the Wall* – and numerous TV tie-in books, including *EastEnders: 20 Years in Albert Square*. He is a regular contributor to the *Guardian*, *Radio Times* and *Gay Times* and lives in London. Rupert Smith's website is www.rupertsmith.org.uk.

D1153526

Service Wash

rupert smith

First published in 2006
by Serpent's Tail, 4 Blackstock Mews, London N4 2BT
website: www.serpentstail.com

Typeset at Neuadd Bwll, Llanwrtyd Wells

Printed by Mackays of Chatham, plc

ISBN: 1-85242-928-3
ISBN-13: 978-1-85242-928-7

10 9 8 7 6 5 4 3 2 1

For Marcus

with thanks to St Jude

prelude: the road to hell

Eileen Weathers awoke early one morning as the first rays of June sunshine filtered through the muslin drapes of her Jacobean-style bedroom, caressing the still-sleeping form of her athletic and much younger husband, Jimmy, who lay beside her. She rose softly so as not to disturb him, tiptoed to the mullioned window and breathed in lungfuls of healthy Essex air softly scented with lilac. She stretched her arms high above her head (yoga) and noted with some pride that her still-firm breasts strained against the flimsy fabric of her nightdress like eager puppies.

Somewhere nearby a blackbird carolled its hymn of joy to the new day. Yes, Mr Blackbird, you're right, thought Eileen. Today is a very good day. And maybe – yes, surely – today is *the* day. The day to begin.

She tripped gaily down the broad hardwood staircase – no creaky boards to avoid there, unlike Nana Scammell's house, where every step was a traitor! – and into the country-style living room. Already the sun was shining through the patio doors and glinting off the crystal-blue waters of the pool, which seemed to laugh 'Come, Eileen! Work can wait!' And indeed she was tempted to throw off her sheer nightie and frolic naked in the caressing coolness. If the ever-present paparazzi got an eyeful, so what? She had nothing to hide. At the age of fifty-five Eileen Weathers was still in the spectacular shape that made her a star in the 1970s.

But no. With iron discipline – the mark of a true professional – she turned away from the beckoning waters and walked purposefully towards the leather-topped desk, where a box-fresh brushed-aluminium PowerBook awaited her touch. She pressed a button, and the machine twanged into life.

Fancy me, she thought, little Eileen Scammell from Elephant and Castle, daughter of an itinerant fish vendor and an occasional seamstress, raised by her Nana in a two-room flat above a pawnbroker's shop on the Walworth Road, using a computer! That's one in the eye for the teachers who wrote me off at the age of fourteen as a thickie, long before they recognised that severe dyslexia combined with attention deficit disorder is often the hallmark of a creative mind.

And what would those teachers say if they knew how much she'd been paid to write a book? Yes, a book. The book it had taken a lifetime of loving and losing to prepare for.

Eileen Weathers was going to write her autobiography.

She paused for a moment, her famously manicured fingers hovering over the keys. Where to begin? With Jimmy, who had brought love into her life when she thought she would never love again? With Charlie Weathers, her first husband, who turned her into a woman? Or with Maggie Parrott, the character she'd played for thirty years as a star of Channel Six's long-running soap, *New Town*? Or with Chocolate and Biscuit, the two silky spaniels who had just burst into the room, their claws clattering on the polished floor? She reached down and caressed their ears as they sat at her feet, gazing up with unquestioning, uncritical adoration, just the way she liked it.

'Where to start, my babies?' she murmured. 'That's the question. Where to start?'

Four simple, loving eyes seemed to hold the answer.

'You're right, children. We'll start at the beginning. That's a very good place to start.'

And so, closing her eyes and taking a deep breath, she put manicured finger to keyboard and let her extraordinary story quite literally spill out.

My name is Eileen Weathers at least that's what they call me now but I was really born a Scammell on my mum's side and Gutteridge on my dads, dad was irish and I went to school round near where we lived Elephant and castle which was in south London where I grew up when I was young. School was boring I never got much eduction but when my dad went away mum always said that he was coming home and my younger brother and sister and me went to live with our nana which was more like a mother and father to me…

chapter one

'Skinscaffolder' was about to get down to virtual business with 'Horny21' when the phone rang, quite disrupting the cyberflow. Horny21, or Paul (thirty-five) as he was known to his mother, hesitated before answering; Skinscaffolder had promised to do some very nasty things to him. But then he considered the fact that the phone had not rung for some weeks, and there were bills to be paid, and so he typed the words 'Fone LOL' and hoped it would keep.

'Paul Mackrell.'

'Paul. Yeah. Hi. Toby Ross. Six Books.'

The words rang like cash registers in Paul's ears, and Skinscaffolder was forgotten.

'Hoping you might be free to do a little job for us.'

'Well, I'm quite busy…' He hit the MUTE button on his keyboard, so that Skinscaffolder's urgent bongs and tinks could not be heard.

'Just a bit of light editing. Fun job.'

'I'll see what I can do. What is it?'

He couldn't afford to play hard to get, because Six Books, the publishing arm of the mighty Channel Six, paid more for a bit of light editing than all Paul's other jobs put together.

'Big celebrity number. Can't tell you too much on the phone.'

'Right…' Paul considered himself to be rather above celebrities.

'But between you and me… I mean, if you're really interested I am authorised to tell you…' Toby lowered his voice to a conspiratorial whisper. 'It's Eileen Weathers.'

It rang no immediate bells. 'Oh.'

'You understand why we need someone discreet.'

'Absolutely.'

'So you're up for it?'

'Obviously it depends on…'

'We'll discuss all that when you come in.'

'Well, I'm quite busy this week with…'

'Friday OK for you? Twelve thirty for a working lunch? Good.'

'Let me see…Friday.' Paul mimed leafing through a diary. 'I should be able to make it. Hmm. Just need to juggle a few things.'

'And in the meantime, keep it shtum, right?'

'Oh, absolutely.'

Toby rang off. Paul immediately phoned a friend.

'Eileen Weathers? Fabulous! I love her. She's a scream. "Ooh, darlin'! The state of her drawers!" Fantastic when she did that rape scene. Will you get to meet Jimmy?'

'Who's Jimmy?'

'God, Paul, don't you know anything? Jimmy Livesey, her real-life husband. I used to fancy him soooooooo much when he was in the show. Put on a bit of weight now, mind you, but I still would. I should be writing this book, not you.'

'Well, don't mention it to anyone just yet. Nothing's signed.'

'Eileen Weathers. You lucky bastard.'

He tried another.

'Well, you must, must, must find out whether it's true or not, because I know someone who used to go out with her in the 1960s and he said she was definitely, definitely a sex change and that everyone knew that she'd been to Casablanca for the operation. Or was it Stockholm?'

He tried another.

'Oh, God, she's Maggie in that awful programme. What's it called? *New Town.* I never watch it. Well, it's just depressing rubbish. I mean, recently there's been this awful storyline about how she's going to lose her council flat, and that miserable daughter of hers has had to come back home so Maggie doesn't know whether to leave Eastgate altogether or just stay and face the music. I mean, it was much better in the old days. Mind you, I did like that young actor. What was his name? Damian something. He was very good. He's done terribly well. I've hardly watched it since he left…'

Paul knew all about Damian Davies, the square-jawed, smooth-skinned man-child adored in dozens of online 'shrines'. The rest he had to google. CLEAN QUEEN WEDS HANDY MAN headed a report from the *Daily Beacon* in 2000. 'Eileen Weathers, forty-nine-year-old star of TV's *New Town*, has tied the knot with younger co-star Jimmy Livesey, thirty. Weathers, best known as Maggie Parrott, manageress of the Clean Queen launderette in the long-running Channel Six soap, said that she and Livesey "want to live like any other newlywed couple" in the star's lavish Essex mansion. Livesey, who joined *New Town* in 1991 as handsome handyman Jason Hamill, would not confirm reports that he is scheduled to leave the show at the end of the year. "Let's just say I've had a lot of interesting offers," said the former football player, "but at the moment there's only one job I'm interested in, and that's being a good husband." Ms Weathers has been married twice before, to actor Charlie Weathers and to builder Brian Champion.'

The *Beacon*'s arch rival, the *Daily Herald*, greeted the happy news in a sour mood. IS IT LEGAL? ran the headline above pictures of 'the newlyweds yesterday' and a grainy picture of a blonde 1960s showgirl with the caption 'Eileen: born a boy?' 'Controversy surrounds the latest "marriage" of *New Town* star Eileen Weathers to toyboy Jimmy Livesey,' ran the uncharitable copy. 'For years, Weathers has been dogged by sex-change rumours dating back to her shady past in sordid Soho strip joints, where she worked under the name Kiki de Londres – hiding her true identity AS A MAN… "It's a publicity stunt that backfired," said Weathers yesterday, laughing off accusations that the "wedding" was invalid. "I made it up as a way of getting attention when I was starting out, and now I can't shake it off. I don't care. All my husbands have known that I'm a real woman."'

And then the trail went cold, apart from a tiny snippet in the *Beacon* from

2002. '*New Town* star Eileen Weathers yesterday won a libel action against the Herald Media Group, publishers of the *Daily Herald*, over a story which cast doubt on the validity of her marriage to former co-star Jimmy Livesey. The *Herald* was ordered to pay damages of £4,000 plus costs. A spokesman for Miss Weathers said that she was happy that justice had been done.'

Later material was long on colour but short on facts. Mr and Mrs Jimmy Livesey welcomed umpteen publications to their Essex home, where the only breath of scandal appeared to be that there was 'no baby joy for Eileen'. A feature in the Beacon's women's pages gave a little biographical information – hard knocks childhood in south-east London, fun and games in the 1960s, sitcoms and soap in the 1970s, a handful of husbands – but concentrated more on skincare regimes. Eileen had 'no fear of washday hands', learned Paul, 'despite spending her working life in TV's most famous launderette, the Clean Queen. "I always moisturise," she says. "Can anyone really afford not to?"'

Paul sighed at the shallowness of it all. What did it matter if Eileen Weathers had lovely hands, or if she'd slept three in a bed during her childhood, or if she was a boy or a girl? Why were people so endlessly fascinated by the minute details of celebrities' lives? Must he really prostitute himself to this kind of second-rate muckraking?

He clicked back on to his chatroom, but Skinscaffolder had got tired of waiting and was now discussing his pole with a more appreciative audience.

There were so many reasons not to take a job like this. Paul's schedule was stretched enough as it was, what with teaching commitments (two full hours a week at a local adult education college, not to mention the preparation) and his own writing. He was, in theory, working hard on the follow-up to his debut novel, *The Frozen Heart*, a poignant coming-of-age story published four years ago to kind reviews and modest sales. His latest creation, a postmodern take on the epistolary novel set in an online chatroom, was nearly half written but seemed to be taking an awful lot of research time. And then there were the screenplays, both of them adaptations of twentieth-century classics that were just waiting for a broadcaster with a bit of vision to snap them up. (At present, both Genet's *Our Lady of the Flowers* and Firbank's *Prancing Nigger* were arrested at the 'treatment' stage.)

Yes, time would certainly be the big factor, thought Paul, fretfully clicking his e-mail to find that his only correspondents were some Russian pornographers and a Nigerian businessman who humbly beseeched his assistance.

Yet what was time but money? His last commission for Six Books, a little number about interior design, had paid enough to buy three clear months of writing time. True, those three months had coincided with a severe case of writer's block, exacerbated by an out-of-control addiction to online sex chat, but that was just bad luck. Another such commission, especially at fancy celebrity prices, could buy the time to write a novel and a screenplay with enough left over, perhaps, to buy the one thing he really needed for his office, a webcam.

He found his diary, buried beneath a pile of newspapers and magazines, and opened it to the current, blank week. '1230,' he wrote on Friday. 'Lunch Toby Ross @ Six. Re Eileen Weathers book.'

For the next ten minutes he stared at this entry. It looked rather good.

The editorial offices of Six Books, publishing wing of the mighty Channel Six, languished in an unsavoury block overlooking an elevated section of the A4 at Hammersmith. Channel Six, with scant respect for the printed word except as a marketing medium, had no hesitation in dumping its unfortunate literati in the middle of a road system, while even the humblest researcher in the core broadcasting business revelled in the super-chic comfort of Six's W1 headquarters.

Paul risked life and limb in a series of underpasses that connected the tube station to the traffic island on which the Six Books block stood. He was half an hour early and was already preparing a line about unpredictable London transport in order to excuse his keenness.

'They're all in a meeting,' said the receptionist once she'd issued him with a security laminate. 'Please take a seat.'

And indeed they were. Toby Ross, editor-in-chief at Six Books and the only person who had actually been there for more than a year, was in consultation with a team of marketing people, design people, research people and salesforce people.

'OK, so *Is Your Husband Queer?* is a runner.' Toby was a man of few words, most of them jargon.

'Check,' said a marketing person.

'Next. Eileen Weathers.'

There was a sharp intake of breath around the table.

'I'm sensing…what?'

'Risky business, Charles,' said a research person. 'Our figures show that *New Town* is on the slip and slide.'

'But Eileen Weathers. Maggie Parrott. You know. "Ooh, darlin'!" Bigger than the show.'

'Ooh, darlin'!' repeated an editorial assistant, who may have been called Camilla, or Sarah, or Fiona, Toby really couldn't remember. Her impersonation of Maggie Parrott's cockney catchphrase sounded Welsh.

'Strong image for POS material, dump bins, posters, instores,' said a salesforce person. 'Walk off the shelves, mate.'

'But the positioning thing,' said Toby. 'Right for us? Right for Six? Is it the icon thing, or the old crumblies thing?'

'Irony,' said a marketing person.

'Yeah, irony. Ironic. Iconic. Hmm…'

'I think, if I might speak,' said Camilla-Sarah-Fiona, 'that she's got a really interesting story and that there's a good chance it would sell quite well, so why not give her a chance and offer her a contract?'

Silence around the table. Toby flipped his pencil deftly across his fingers.

'The thing is, right…'

'Yah?'

'Ancient history, mate. She's got the contract. She's delivered.'

'Oh.' Camilla-Sarah-Fiona furrowed her brow in thought. This was not something she did often, as you could see from the peachy smoothness of her skin. 'So she's got a contract, she's written a book…'

'Correct.' The rest of the team watched her labouring towards publishing awareness.

C-S-F smiled. 'So now you can publish it! That's great.'

'Wrong!' said Toby. 'Not just a question of writing it and publishing it.

Otherwise all these well-paid people—' he gestured around the table '—would be out of a job.'

'Oh.'

'It's about the positioning, the brand, the market, the wider picture, trends, er, the consumer thing,' said Toby.

'Right.' C-S-F was writing these words down, as if taking dictation.

'Also,' said Toby, 'there's a slight hitch in that what she's delivered is absolute fucking crap.'

'Is that a problem, Toby?' asked a design person.

'Needn't be, with the right cover,' said the marketing person. 'Got some good pics?'

'Course, mate,' said Toby. 'Wouldn't have commissioned it without good pics.'

'Got a good title?'

'How about *Maggie 'n' Me*?'

'Sounds lezzie.'

'*It Isn't All Soap*.'

'Don't get it…'

'*Many Weathers*.'

'Yeah…I see…Getting there, getting there…'

'How about just *Eileen*?'

'What, *Just Eileen* or just *Eileen*?'

'Just *Eileen*.'

'I'm loving that.'

The title was written down on several pieces of paper. A design person started thinking fonts.

'So it's only the words on the pages that are the problem?'

'Yeah,' laughed Toby. 'But that we can fix. I've got a writer coming in…'

At the word 'writer', the team looked benignly curious, as if Toby had just said 'giant panda' or 'Amazonian head-shrinker'. C-S-F actually went 'Aaaaw!'

'Job done,' said the marketing person. 'Just a question of commitment. How much advance did you give her?'

'Well…' Toby wasn't particularly pleased to be asked this, as for once he had been bettered by an agent. 'Obviously, for a star of her calibre – and as you said we are talking icon here – we had to go tops in an auction situation…'

The team was waiting.

'So we'd definitely be looking for a return on an investment of two-fifty k.'

'Two-fifty k,' murmured the marketing person, hastily scribbling figures. 'OK. So you need a guaranteed sale of at least 500,000 copies at a cover price of, say £19.99.'

'Crikey,' said C-S-F, to whom this sounded an awful lot.

'Yup.'

There was a minute's meditation.

'Better have a really good cover, then,' said the design person.

That seemed to clinch it.

'So Eileen is a runner, then?' said Toby.

Camilla-Sarah-Fiona squirmed with delight in her chair, knowing that she'd just seen real publishing business done. 'Ooh, darlin',' she said.

After an hour, the receptionist looked up from her magazine and told Paul that someone was on the way to collect him.

It was Camilla-Sarah-Fiona.

'Hi,' she said, extending a hand. 'I'm Emma. You're the writer.' She was rather excited to meet one at last, especially one that so looked the part. He was of medium height, fragile build, thinning gingerish hair, glasses (of course) and a general air of sexless intelligence. She had never seen anyone like this. The boys Emma knew were called things like Guy and Jamie and played rugby. Paul Mackrell the writer was very different indeed, and would make for interesting dinner-party conversation. 'His skin was so pale,' she would say, 'as if he didn't get outdoors much…I suppose they don't.'

Upstairs, Toby greeted Paul with the same boisterous bonhomie that he extended to all men whom he suspected of being homosexual. 'Good to see you, mate. You've met…'

'Emma. Yes.'

'Yeah. Emma is going to be your project editor. Get the teas in, Emms, there's a good girl.'

'Right away.'

Toby swivelled his chair around and looked out over the traffic. 'So, Paul. Eileen Weathers. Iconic. Ironic. Yeah?'

'A very interesting woman, by all accounts.'

Toby swivelled back. 'Yeah?' He looked genuinely surprised. 'You said it, mate. Great book, big priority for us, big Christmas sales…'

'You mean Christmas of next year, do you?'

Toby laughed. 'Nice one, mate! Those were indeed the days. So obviously delivering the finished copy by September at the latest…'

It was July.

'What exactly needs to be done?'

'Like I said on the phone, bit of a wash and brush-up. Nothing you can't handle.'

He pulled out a flimsy A4 file and dropped it on the desk. It made, on impact, barely a thud.

'What's that?'

'That's the manuscript, mate.'

'A sample chapter?' Paul picked it up; there were at most sixty pages.

'Might need a bit of padding here and there, but basically that's it.'

'But surely you can't be…'

'You'll be wanting to know about the budget.'

'I'm more concerned about the…'

'And because this is such a priority for us, we're obviously talking way above the usual rate.'

Paul stopped weighing the manuscript and prepared to drive a hard bargain. He had talked it over with friends, and absolutely no way was he going to accept less than £3,500 for the job – especially now that he'd seen how much work it involved.

'OK.'

There was a pause while the two men eyeballed each other. Toby was the healthy, handsome, married type that Paul usually wanted to please, but not under these circumstances.

They both spoke at once.

'So how much would you be…?'

'What sort of figures…?'

There was another silence. Paul was about to shape his lips to say the words 'three and a half thousand', but Toby beat him to it.

'Ten k max. Can't go any higher than that.'

Paul swallowed hard and tried to look crestfallen. 'Oh, right. Well, I suppose I'll find a way of doing it for that. I don't know if it's possible, though. It's a lot of work.'

'Sorry, mate. Ten tops. I'd hate to have to give it to someone else. We need a safe pair of hands on this one.'

Paul thought of all the writing time that £10,000 could buy.

'It's a deal,' he said, holding out a long, pale, Aubrey Beardsley hand.

They shook, each man feeling he had got the better of the other.

Paul was still shaking when he got home, and was so excited that he didn't even check his e-mail. He almost phoned a friend to tell him that he was actually holding in his hands some pieces of paper that had emanated from the famously manicured fingers of Eileen 'Ooh, darlin'!' Weathers. But then his eyes fell on the first paragraph and his blood ran cold.

My name is Eileen Weathers at least that's what they call me now but I was really born a Scammell on my mum's side and Gutteridge on my dads…

He scanned down the page; the paragraph continued. He flipped over to page two. Still no indents. He flicked through the entire manuscript – all sixty single-sided, double-spaced pages of it – and realised, with dread, that this wasn't so much just one chapter, or even one section – this was just one paragraph.

Looking on the bright side, there were at least some full stops, although not all of them were where they should have been.

And then he did something that, under normal circumstances, he would never do. He turned to the last page.

> ...under the bed all the time. When Charlie found out about this he was NOT AMUSED but looking back on it now he was a fine one to talk as he was quite capable of pollishing off a bottle of whiskey a day if not two so that put everything into perspective. And when the divorce came through we are good friends to this day which I always think is best and his daughter

It ended halfway down a page. No full stop. Nothing more. In a state bordering on panic, Paul called Emma, who had declared herself 'ready to answer any questions you may have'.

'Where's the rest of it?'

'I'll have to ask Toby.'

'He said that this was all there was.'

'I expect it is, then.'

'But you know the end?'

'The end...? Well...'

'Where it just – well, stops?'

'Oh, yes. The end.'

'Didn't it strike you as rather odd? I mean, is she trying to do something clever? It's not some kind of literary device, is it?'

'That must be it.'

'You're sure there aren't more pages?'

'I'll have to ask Toby.'

'But Toby said there weren't.'

'Well, then.'

'Can you get in touch with the agent?'

Emma's voice went high and, Paul thought, tearful.

'Oh, gosh, well we're very busy at the moment and actually, no, I think that's not really something that we can do from here.'

'Can Toby do it?'

'The thing is, Toby's on holiday now until September.'

'Did he leave any notes?'

'I'd have to ask him.'

'Did you take any notes when you read it?'

'Well,' said Emma, suddenly in a hurry, 'I'll e-mail you the agent's number. Thanks a lot for that, Paul. Sounds as if it's going fine. Don't hesitate to call if there's anything more I can do.'

Paul opened his internet connection and spent the rest of the afternoon in furious conversation with more than a dozen other housebound gentlemen with overactive imaginations.

As a university graduate, and the proud holder of not only a BA but also a PhD, Paul was not afraid of research – and so, that evening, he did something that he had never willingly done before. He sat down in front of his television, and he watched a soap opera.

He watched the whole thing, from the appalling cod-reggae theme song ('Life is what you make it/In a new town…Friends are round the corner/In a new town') right through to the closing credits. He felt, for twenty-seven minutes, as if he had arrived uninvited at a party where he knew nobody, wrongly dressed and possibly in a foreign country. During the first half, before the commercial break, he was fairly certain that he hadn't seen Eileen Weathers or her screen incarnation, Maggie Parrott. The action centred around an interfering old woman with a posh voice who was making strident demands of anyone she encountered, apparently related to a compost bin. There was a puzzling scene in which a young mixed-race teenager talked to a friendly teacher about his truancy problem and realised that it was really a good idea to go back to school. There was some concern about an elderly gentleman's prostate, and then, just before the ads, there was a scene in which all the characters were black.

During the adverts, Paul leafed through the *Daily Herald*, which trumpeted NEW TOWN, OLD HAT! in a headline on page four before telling its readers that 'It's time for Channel Six's old warhorse to be put out to pasture! Viewing figures last month reached an all-time low of six million – the LOWEST since the show started in 1976! It's a far cry from the days when over 30 million tuned in to watch Maggie and Ron tie the knot in 1979. Six bosses say there are currently "no plans whatsoever" to axe the underperforming soap…'

But then he suddenly paid attention. The adverts were over, the posh old lady was making her way towards a sordid parade of shops – and there in the middle of the row was a launderette. Paul knew next to nothing about popular culture, but even he knew that Maggie Parrott was synonymous with the Clean Queen launderette in the fictional new-town estate of Eastgate. She had been since his childhood. It was a fact hard to avoid.

The posh lady neared the Clean Queen, which appeared from the exterior to be empty – but as soon as she was indoors it became quite full of non-speaking characters. And who was this, emerging from behind a soap-dispensing machine?

"Ello, Poppy. Service wash?'

'No, Margaret. I've come about these compost bins.'

'Ooh, darlin',' said Maggie, for it was she. 'I don't want nothing to do with them. Dirty things.'

'But that's just it, my dear,' started the one called Poppy, a tweedy old dear who could have played Miss Marple. Paul didn't listen to her speech about waste reduction and concentrated instead on Maggie's blue nylon housecoat, her blonde hair set in a style that had not been fashionable since the early 1980s, her full theatrical warpaint, her famously manicured hands that were never chipped or chapped. Illiterate to the point of idiocy she may have been, but there was no doubt, thought Paul, that the woman was a star.

'…what with Dean and all his troubles, I shan't have a great deal of time to think about it, but I can see that it's important for all of us to try and reduce waste if we can.'

'Thank you, Margaret, my dear. I knew I could count on you.'

'Ooh, darlin', you wouldn't be the first and I don't suppose you shall be the last.'

The slot was running to its close, and there was just time for the cliffhanger scene (it was, as the doctor feared, cancer of the prostate) before the nauseating theme song jangled back into life and a bullying announcer commanded Paul to watch a programme called *Path Lab* that followed 'next on Six'.

'Shan't!' said Paul, with uncharacteristic skittishness, and turned the television off.

Less than a week later Paul was met at a quiet commuter station in semi-rural Essex by a young man whom he would have paid good money, had he had it, to meet. He was about five foot eight, a little shorter than Paul, but gave the impression of being bigger by dint of broad shoulders, powerful arms and sturdy legs. He had close-cropped black hair, a flattened nose, a scarred eyebrow and the surly, swarthy looks that appeal without fail to intellectual gentlemen. Paul thought for a moment that he recognised him, but then realised, with a flush of embarrassment, that these were the exact looks he had conjured up for his imaginary friend, Skinscaffolder.

'I'm Danny.' He had a warm, dry grip. 'You're the writer, right?'

'Paul Mackrell.'

Danny did something athletic that propelled him over the car bonnet – it was a white Mercedes, naturally – and opened the passenger door.

'Jump in. The old dear's expecting you.'

Paul had a rush of celebrity adrenalin when he heard Eileen Weathers – a national icon – referred to as 'the old dear'. He imagined doing this at the dinner parties to which he was already being invited on the strength of this new commission.

Danny's denim-encased thigh was temptingly close as Paul fumbled with the safety belt; already the car was speeding out of the station forecourt. Fast cars and handsome men always made Paul feel reckless.

'You're not the husband, then?'

'Fuck, no. Wouldn't want his job, mate! I'm just the minder.'

'Oh, I see. And have you worked with Miss Weathers long?'

'Feels like all my life. And for God's sake don't call her Miss Weathers.'

'What should I call her? Mrs Livesey?'

'Just call her Eileen.'

'And what do you call her, Danny?' Paul hadn't flirted like this since his twenties (not that it was successful then either).

'Depends if she's behaving herself.'

'And if she's not?'

'You don't wanna hear, mate, believe me.' Danny flashed a set of carnivorous gnashers at Paul and threw the car into a stomach-turning swerve. The entrance was so concealed that Paul screamed, thinking they were ploughing into a hedge. Tyres crunched on gravel and the car stopped.

'Nervous type, eh?' Danny reached across and massaged Paul's shoulder. 'Relax, mate. You're in safe hands.'

Before Paul could fling himself into Danny's manly arms, the car door was open.

'Ring the bell. Someone'll let you in.'

The white Mercedes disappeared with its tempting cargo.

The house, set back from the road behind a thick screen of Lawsonia, was the 'lavish Essex mansion' of press reports. Like all extremely expensive buildings, it combined maximum surface area with minimum height; for most of the time it was just a sprawling bungalow. Wings stretched to left and right of a porticoed door, all painted white, with clipped box trees in aluminium pots on either side. There was an old-fashioned bell-pull to the right which set off a discreetly musical chime somewhere in the deep, rich interior. Paul waited and wished he'd put on a tie.

Dogs barked, doors slammed and a shape moved beyond the frosted-glass panes. 'That's enough, Biscuit! Get down!' It was a mellifluous, cultivated woman's voice.

The door opened, and there stood another flunkie – how many did she have? – a somewhat scruffy woman in a wool skirt and silk blouse. She had salt-and-pepper hair and a clean, wrinkled face. This, presumed Paul, was the secretary – and he immediately felt sorry for the poor woman who had been obliged to type, print and send out the subliterate ramblings of the manuscript.

'Oh, good afternoon, you must be Mr Mackrell,' she said in a voice that instantly placed her as the genteel, down-on-her-luck type that was obliged to pander to flashy rich folk like Eileen Weathers. 'Please, do come in.'

The entrance hall was covered in extremely expensive dark parquet. There were a few enormous *objets d'art* strategically placed by an interior designer; no ordinary person had such good taste, let alone an actress.

'I'm sure Mrs Livesey won't keep you long,' said the secretary. She picked up her glasses, dangling on a gold chain around her neck, and consulted a small pocketbook. 'She's having her daily massage just at present. Perhaps I could show you into the living room.'

'Thank you,' said Paul, agog at the idea of a TV star having a daily massage just yards away. They walked past a kitchen, a music room and a dining room, whence came the scent of an enormous bunch of lilies.

'Mrs Livesey adores lilies,' said the secretary with a sigh, 'but they don't half stain.'

The writer's instinct for dialogue picked up the verbal quirk. Ah, thought Paul proudly, she's bettered herself.

'Here we are,' said the secretary, gesturing around a living room the size of a small playing field, where there were three enormous leather sofas like cattle grazing on sheepskin rugs. 'The lounge.'

'It's lovely,' said Paul.

He felt the secretary's eyes boring into him and wondered if he ought to have tipped her.

'Will Miss...er, Mrs Livesey be long?'

There was a long silence; the secretary smiled inscrutably, and Paul began to feel uncomfortably hot.

And then she laughed and whipped off her glasses with one well-manicured hand.

'Ooh, darlin'!' she said in a familiar cockney twang. 'And the fucking critics say I can't act!'

chapter two

'And I'm telling you that nobody is interested in bloody compost bins.'

'Well, thank you for that, Michael. The research suggests that environmental-stroke-green issues are important or very important to over sixty per cent of viewers.'

'For Christ's sake, Tracey, read the reviews! "*New Town*'s recent storylines are as stale as Poppy Ditchling's compost bucket." I quote.'

'Well, of course Poppy's bucket is stale. I mean, that's the whole point. I think the message is getting across.'

We join a *New Town* script conference *in medias res*. Tracey Reynolds, series producer of the moment, is fighting her corner against veteran writer Michael Hawker. His is a lone voice of dissent (the rest fear, rightly, for their jobs), but he speaks for all.

'Where's the drama in a fucking compost bin, Trace?'

'I've warned you about language, Mike.'

'And I've told you a thousand times that only middle-class ponces are called Mike. It's Mick or Michael to you.'

'The fact remains that Poppy's recycling story is absolutely key to our mid- to long-term strategy as agreed at the last quarterly meeting…'

'Quarterly bollocks. There won't be a mid term for this show, let alone a long term, if we don't get some drama back into it.'

'Oh, and I suppose by drama you mean rape and murder and suchlike.'

'At least in those days we got viewers,' said Michael, whose idea of 'drama' had been formed by too many viewings of *The Godfather*.

Tracey flicked through a file. 'And I would remind you that in those days we got complaints from the Broadcasting Standards Authority about excessive violence in a pre-watershed slot.'

'So what, Tracey? Are we doomed to a future of potato peelings and energy-saving lightbulbs?'

'Don't be ridiculous. We've got Dr D's prostate cancer; that's a slow burn. We've got the whole issue of Rooksfield District Council selling off its housing stock…'

'Christ on a fucking bike,' said Michael, who longed to introduce such colourful phrases into *New Town* scripts but was obliged instead to save them for meetings. 'I must be in the wrong conference. This is *New Town* we're talking about, isn't it, not *Teletubbies*? I remember this show, Tracey, when we had conflict and controversy. Tell me, have you been secretly hired by the opposition to get us closed down?'

'Michael, if only your scripts were as hilariously funny as you are, maybe the actors would have something to get their teeth into.'

'There's nothing wrong with my scripts…'

And so it continued for a further twenty minutes until sandwiches were brought in. Tracey Reynolds was not having a happy time as *New Town* producer, a job that even industry friends described as a poisoned chalice. She had been brought in from documentary features, a department in which she had ridden the crest of the reality TV wave through no particular merit of her own, and had been given the impossible brief of a) getting *New Town*'s viewing figures back up to their high watermark and b) avoiding at all costs further censure from the watchdogs. As she had neither the integrity nor the intelligence to realise that this was an impossibility, she had taken the job, and floundered. The writers were in more or less open rebellion. The actors sniggered behind her back and had started making increasingly bizarre requests for leave. The scheduling department was up in arms, as every attempt to plan a day's shooting was scuppered by someone being at their daughter's school open day, or undergoing dental treatment, or doing panto. And still the viewing figures were sliding, the reviews were carping and the only headlines *New Town* got were due to the scandalous misbehaviour of the cast. Tracey got little support from her superiors at Channel Six and none at all from her immediate boss, head of drama Nick Needs, who had long since stopped answering calls or coming to meetings, almost as if he were trying to distance himself from the show.

The biggest thorn in Tracey's side were the actors. T. J. Daniels, who played Maggie's window-cleaner boyfriend Vince, was in the news once again for romancing women less than half his age (he was fifty-four; the latest girlfriend was nineteen). It had seemed such a good idea at the time to hire a washed-up rock star with acting ambitions; now they were paying the price. Then there were Tyrone, Leah and Gemma, the *New Town* bratpack, brought in as a job lot to appeal to the teen demographic and fulfilling their professional destiny by developing serious drug habits. Even worse was the Steve Seddon situation; it could only be a matter of time before that photographer in Earl's Court released his 'physique studies' of the show's resident hunk to a slavering press. All of this Tracey had kept the lid on – just – and they had the nerve to criticise her storylines.

'Now, if we can get down to some work,' she said through a mouthful of egg and cress, 'I'd like to move Maggie on a bit. Who's got some ideas?'

'How about killing the old bag off in a freak tumble-drying accident?'

'Be serious, Mike.'

'I am serious. She's way past her sell-by date. Come on, does anybody really enjoy writing for Maggie any more?'

The rest of the writers looked down at their doodle-pads.

'Thanks for the support, guys. But there's nothing more for her to do. She's done everything. Her story is over. It's time she took a taxi.'

'Maggie Parrott will always be part of *New Town*. She's the figurehead.'

'And that's the problem. She's identified with the past. She's old, she's tired and, let's face it, Eileen Weathers isn't the world's greatest actress.'

'Michael, this isn't up for discussion,' said Tracey.

'That's not what it says here,' said Michael, pulling a memo from his file. '"All ideas gratefully received…"'

'Well, not that one.'

'Why not? Because Nick Needs says so?'

Tracey longed to say: 'Michael – you're fired.' But she wasn't allowed to do that either – because Nick Needs said so.

'Subject closed. I'd like to hear any serious ideas for Maggie.'

But ideas, serious or otherwise, came there none. And Michael was right: in nearly thirty years, Maggie had done everything, and had everything done to her. She arrived in Eastgate in 1976 – in the first-ever episode of *New Town* – as a homeless single mother struggling to raise her little daughter Hayley, the product of a long-distant rape. She moved in with her domineering mother Joyce, got a job in the Clean Queen launderette and fought tooth and nail to keep herself decent. Then she met and fell in love with a nice local lad, Ron Parrott, whom she married (in front of those famous 30 million viewers) in 1979. Their union was blessed by twins, Andrew and Amanda.

The 1980s had not been kind to the Parrotts. Ron lost his job and his self-respect while Maggie, by now manageress of the Clean Queen, came to terms with being a breadwinner. In more prosperous times, they bought their council house only to see the market crash in 1988. Little wonder that an exhausted Maggie sought solace in the arms of new arrival Bernard Johnson, a *New Town* novelty insofar as he was black. Their union was blessed, or maybe cursed, by tearaway tot Dean, whom Ron dutifully raised as his own despite the obvious difference in skin colour and the hurtful remarks at the Eastgate Arms.

When Ron dropped dead, Maggie started a wild affair with Jason Hamill, the handsome handyman. Since then she'd lost her mother and her older son, she'd seen her older daughter marry the local doctor and then get raped in her turn (things tended to be cyclical in *New Town*), her younger daughter get hooked on crack (just like the actress who played her) and her love child Dean playing truant, to almost universal indifference. On the bright side she'd found companionship with the local window-cleaner Vince, a union that came far too late in the day to be blessed with anything much at all.

Michael was right: short of involving Maggie in some kind of bizarre illness or accident, her story was all played out. But it was hard to imagine

New Town without her – and Tracey didn't have that much imagination. She was also rightly afraid of Eileen Weathers's agent.

'Maggie is the linchpin,' said Tracey. 'It's up to you guys to find stories for her. I don't want to hear words like "won't" or "can't". You're employed to have ideas, not to…not have ideas.'

'OK,' said a new writer. 'How about if Maggie responds to Poppy's recycling initiative by making the launderette environmentally friendly? You know, from Clean Queen to Green Queen.'

'I like that,' said Tracey.

'Somebody shoot me,' said Michael.

'Michael, your turn,' said Tracey. 'You've made it perfectly clear what we shouldn't be doing. Now I'm sure you'd like to tell us all what we should be doing.'

'Just look at what's going on in real new towns today,' said Michael. 'Teenagers have a nine o'clock curfew because they're running out of control. They're having sex at twelve, thirteen, and they're smoking crack by fourteen. Women like Maggie are being mugged in their own streets…'

'We've done drugs, we've done juvenile delinquency, we've pioneered storylines about schoolgirl mums, and if you think I'm going to have some little oik bashing Maggie over the head in Lapwing Close then you're very much mistaken. So, Ben. Green Queen – I like where you're going with that. It's fresh, it's topical…'

Michael, who knew when he was beaten, started drawing a hangman's noose on his doodle-pad.

Readers who have been abroad for the last thirty years may not be familiar with *New Town* – although there's really no excuse, because it now shows on cable services all over the world – so it would be as well to recap a little bit of TV history.

New Town was born in 1976, a very good year for British TV (*Rock Follies*, *I, Claudius*), in response to a perceived gap in the market for popular drama aimed at a southern working-class audience. Set in the fictional new town of Rooksfield, it featured a disparate bunch of uprooted Londoners and indigenous posh folk who found themselves cheek by jowl in the suburb of Eastgate, once a charming rural village, now a model housing estate that had absorbed the very few buildings that the 1960s planners really couldn't knock down. Eastgate, said the producers, was a microcosm of British society in the 1970s, by which they meant that there were two different accents, one skin tone and no queers. Life revolved around the pub, the corner shop and, of course, the launderette – because where would popular drama be if everyone owned a washing machine?

In those far-off days, exteriors were shot on film in a real housing estate in west London, while everything else was done in the studio, which caused a bumpy time in the continuity department. In the 1980s, riding high on those 30 million viewers, Channel Six coughed up the money to build a brand-new Eastgate on a brown-field site in Bromley, whither, to their horror, the actors were obliged to travel every day. The 'production village' was worse than the worst new town, but it had the great advantage of being cheap.

The drama originally centred around the clash between the old posh folk (Dr and Mrs Lazarus Ditchling) and the new, brash cockneys (battle-axe Joyce Haywood, her daughter Maggie and *her* illegitimate offspring Hayley). Worlds collided in the Eastgate Arms, names were called and slaps exchanged, but eventually the Ditchlings and the Haywoods came to realise that, after all, people are people, and reached a truce in time for Maggie's triumphant wedding in 1979. Since then, *New Town* had struggled to keep up the drama – but by the 1980s it was a habit that the viewing public found hard to shake. It attempted to reflect the society around it, but always five years too late. An Asian family took over the corner shop in 1983, there was an Aids storyline in 1990 and as the thirtieth anniversary loomed there were suggestions that the show might tackle asylum-seekers.

Along the way, *New Town* had created many stars who twinkled for a while then, mostly, burned out. Eileen Weathers remained – a little eclipsed but still shining. Dr and Mrs Ditchling were still there from the old days and were expected to die in harness at any moment. The rest of the original cast had left, been sacked, died or, as was the case with Maggie's daughter Hayley, morphed into different actors.

Currently, the billings in the TV listings mags looked something like this.

7.30pm New Town

Some bad news for Dr Lazarus, while Maggie finds out more about recycling.

Maggie Parrott	Eileen Weathers
Dr Lazarus Ditchling	Terence Lee
Poppy Ditchling	Marjorie Mayhew
Dr David Ditchling	Tim Boreham
Hayley Ditchling	Tricia Marvell
Vince Palmer	T. J. Daniels
Bernard Johnson	Benjamin Oluwatobi
Dean Parrott	Tyrone D
Amanda Parrott	Leah Wilkinson
Dawn Stannard-Watson	Gemma Leeds
Dave Stannard-Watson	Steve Seddon

Episode written by Ben McKenna
Producer Tracey Reynolds
For more cast see Wednesday

Soon, these characters will seem as familiar to you as they already are to millions of addicted viewers who tune in four times a week to watch 'those New Towners', as the announcers call them.

But even though *New Town* was still going after thirty years, it was a far-from-happy show. Tracey Reynolds was the fifteenth producer to sit in the hotseat and had already lasted longer than her two predecessors. Whenever *New Town* hit a bad patch, a head had to roll – and traditionally it was the producer's.

So concerned were Channel Six about their flagship show that a culture of secrecy and paranoia had grown up around the Bromley lot, something akin to East Berlin in the last days of Communist rule. There were shredders in every office, into which employees were obliged to feed even the most innocent piece of paper. Cleaning staff were vetted to a degree not normally seen outside MI5, just in case they were tabloid spies – which, nevertheless, some of them still were. The actors were ruled by contracts that threatened instant dismissal if they discussed the show even with friends, while the senior production staff lived in hermetic isolation, unable to socialise just in case drink should loosen their tongues. The press office had become an Orwellian ministry of truth, issuing denials, counter-statements and lies in order to throw up a smokescreen around the show's increasingly banal storylines. There was an annual battle between *New Town* and the press to conceal or reveal the 'big' Christmas storyline. One year, so much sensational stuff had been leaked that the producers were obliged to broadcast a Christmas Day show in which all the characters had a perfectly nice time. Ratings dipped below 8 million for the first time in *New Town*'s history, as viewers turned over to watch a teenage girl being carved up with the turkey knife in a rival family show.

Eileen Weathers rose above it all with the hauteur of an actress who knows she is bigger than the show. They couldn't sack her – there would be a public outcry, not to mention an enormous settlement negotiated by her Rottweiler agent. The show wouldn't fold – Channel Six had far too much of an investment for that, and advertising revenue remained high – and so as long as Eileen could jog along to her not-so-distant retirement, she wouldn't complain. She'd got a lot out of *New Town* – fame, fortune, a nice house or two, not to mention a much younger husband – and still they needed her more than she needed them.

In times of trouble, it was always to Eileen that they turned, knowing that the public loved her no matter what. She had been around so long she was part of the national landscape. She was a totem, a touchstone. And so, in the wider scheme of things, it was important to Channel Six that Eileen Weathers should publish an autobiography just now. It would remind people how much they liked her, and how much they owed to *New Town* for having given them such a warm and wonderful person. The book would sell a few copies, which never hurt, but more to the point it would spark an orgy of *New Town* nostalgia just in time for the thirtieth anniversary. It would strengthen *New Town*'s hold on the nation's affections, not to mention bolstering Six's chances come the next round of franchise renewals.

And so – although neither Paul Mackrell nor Eileen Weathers realised it at the time – there was more riding on their collaboration than met the eye.

chapter three

Seven hours after his arrival in Essex, Paul was on the last train back to London, his head spinning, his eyes burning and his bag stuffed with cassette tapes containing an oral history of Eileen Weathers. He dreaded the task of transcribing, yet he knew that he had the kernel of a perfectly serviceable showbiz memoir, if unlikely to win any prizes. He would need to visit again, of course: there were so many questions still to be asked, not to mention the overwhelming attraction of Danny the minder, who had driven him back to the station wearing only a pair of grease-stained cut-offs ('I've been fixing the Porsche') and a smelly old T-shirt of indeterminate colour.

Paul's dreams that night were a curious collage of Eileen's Essex mansion, her spicy anecdotes, odd fragments from *New Town* (in which, Paul discovered, he had been unexpectedly cast, without a script and frequently without trousers) – and endless visions of Danny lowering himself on to the dreamer's face.

Paul awoke, dry-mouthed and scarcely refreshed, made himself a pint of espresso and got straight down to work. This was unheard of, as any of Paul's self-employed peers will understand. But these were no ordinary interviews: these were the ramblings of a major TV star.

This is what he heard:

Paul: I'm going to have to ask you when exactly you were born.

Eileen: (*coyly*) I'm not sure that I really want to answer that question, darlin'.

Paul: I'm afraid you're going to have to…

Eileen: What a gentleman! Oi, Danny! He wants to know when I was born!

Danny: (*off*) Shall I put cyanide in his coffee, Ei?

Eileen: Pay no attention to Danny, dear…That's it, love, pop it down on the table and then leave us alone. I don't want you hearing all my secrets.

Danny: I know 'em already, don't I?

Eileen: You don't know the half of it, darlin'. That's it, run along. (*to Paul*) Yes, he has got a nice bum, hasn't he?

Paul: Oh, I…

Eileen: You don't have to be embarrassed with me. (*touches Paul's leg in motherly fashion*) I've seen it all before.

Paul: I bet you have.

Eileen: Second of November 1951. There. That wasn't so bad. I hope that thing of yours is recording, because I'm never going to repeat those words.

Paul: (*checking*) Yes, it's working.

Eileen: Second of November 1951, there I go again. That makes me fifty-four years old, although you don't have to labour the point, do you? Let them work it out for themselves.

Paul: And tell me where you were born.

Eileen: Oh, I've done all that already, haven't I?

Paul: It wasn't actually in the manuscript that I received.

Eileen: Are you sure? Well, I'm sure it was meant to be. But I suppose I got carried away with all the other stories. I do have a tendency to run away with myself sometimes and skate over the facts.

Paul: Yes…

Eileen: You don't have to agree with me, darlin'. Anyway, where was I?

Oh, yes. My noble birth. (*assumes posh accent*) I was born with a silver spoon in me mouth, don't you know?

Paul: I'm sure.

Eileen: All right, it's a fair cop. I was born in the Elephant and Castle, which back in them days wasn't exactly the smartest address that a girl could have. My mum took in mending, which just about kept a roof over our heads, although every week there was a battle with the landlord when he came round to collect the rent. Well, of course we didn't have council flats in them days. We lived on whatever we could earn, and if we didn't have it we couldn't spend it. I learned that from my mother. Not like kids today, who seem to have lost any idea of the value of money...

There followed several minutes on today's credit economy, and a lengthy encomium on Mother's frugality, her cleverness with a needle and her love for life, qualities that Eileen believed she had inherited.

Eileen: All the Scammells, that's my mother's family, were from south London, so there were lots of cousins and aunts and uncles around during my childhood. They were what I would call decent working-class people, in that they always kept themselves nice and they never asked nobody for a handout. Not like some of the riff-raff who came into the street in their dressing gowns and slippers and never had a pot to piss in. We were a cut above them even if it was hard for Mum to make ends meet sometimes.

Paul: What about your father's family?

Eileen: They weren't so much a part of my childhood really...

Paul: You don't mention your father very much in your, er, book.

Eileen: No, and I think that's probably for the best.

Paul: But I'm afraid we're going to have to say something about him. People are going to wonder where you came from.

Eileen: Well, it wasn't a virgin birth if that's what you're thinking. Far from it, dear…Let's just say that Daddy was…away for most of my childhood.

Paul: Who was he, though?

Eileen: His name was Edward Gutteridge.

Paul: And what was he like?

Eileen: Pass.

Paul: I mean, what did he look like?

Eileen: I don't really know, dear. Mum had a couple of photos…

Paul: You mean you didn't know your father?

Eileen: Correct. (*long pause*)

Paul: If this is something you'd rather come back to later…

Eileen: No, we've got to face up to it, I suppose. Daddy left before I was a year old. He was…well, he was a travelling man, let's leave it at that.

Paul: Were he and your mother married?

Eileen: Oh, yes. I'm not a bastard.

Paul: I didn't mean…

Eileen: Don't worry, darlin'! I'm just teasing you! No, they were married all right, and Mum said it was the worst mistake of her life, which probably explains why I've had a few troubles in that area myself. It wasn't exactly a good role model for a young girl, was it? 'Daddy buggered off and left us before you were a year old, dear. Probably didn't love us enough. Probably your fault.'

Paul: So, your brothers and sisters…

Eileen: Oh, you don't miss a trick, do you? Well, that's your job, I suppose, catching me out, winkling the truth out of me. Yes, my darling brother Keith and my precious little sister Rose were born seven and ten years later than me respectively. As for their fathers, well, that's something I'd rather not go into, because this is my story, not theirs. That's something they have to come to terms with in their own way, do you know what I mean?

Paul: Of course.

Eileen: So even though I grew up as Eileen Gutteridge, I always thought of myself as a Scammell, because they were such warm, lovely people…

Next came a paean to the spirit of old south London, forged in the heat of war, strengthened by adversity, all in it together and so on. Paul didn't feel that any of this would be useful and didn't bother to write it down. If necessary he could make up some suitable rubbish at a later date.

Then she got on to sex.

Eileen: …and certainly no shortage of boyfriends. Well, I loved the local lads, to be honest, and I still do. I've never gone for the posh type with airs and graces, although I've had my fair share of opportunity, oh, yes. But I like 'em rough and tough and down to earth.

Paul: Mmm…

Eileen: Ooh, you like a bit of rough as well, do you, darlin'? Well, we're going to get along famously, aren't we? So by the time I was living with my Nana Scammell down in Walworth, there were always gentleman callers. And they were gentlemen in those days. They'd pick you up for a date, and they'd bring a little something for Nana, which was kind, because the poor old thing didn't get out much and she appreciated the attention. She'd been a bit of a raver in her time, you know, back in the 1800s or whenever it was that she was young. She flirted with them like mad, even though I told her she'd get a lot further if she put her teeth in before answering the door. So, yes, boys, boys, boys…

Paul: You said in the manuscript that some of them were on the wrong side of the law.

Eileen: Oh, my God, you can say that again! I mean, south London in the '60s, darlin'…We were on Richardson turf. They were the Krays' big rivals. Smashing lads.

Paul: So the stories about you being a gangsters' moll…

Eileen: All true, every bit of them, and there's things that I could talk about that would get me a gun to the head even forty years on. But I never saw that side of things. As a lady you were protected. They treated us like princesses, always bought us nice presents, and our job was to look pretty and keep our mouths shut. Years later I read about some of the stuff that was going on and I just couldn't believe it. I mean, I knew those lads. Some of them I knew very well indeed. And I still think that there was a conspiracy to get them put away. The cops were very bent, you know…

It was on the tip of Paul's tongue to ask if (as had been suggested) Eileen had ever been a) on the game or b) an accessory to violent crime, but he decided that, for now, it was more important to win her trust. But those 'presents' to Nana Scammell…those nights out with notorious south London mobsters…For now, however, he contented himself with Eileen's rose-tinted memories of her misspent youth.

Eileen: And you see that's what I've always looked for in a man: I like them to be men. Not some poofy ponce – no offence, dear – but a real man who knows how to treat a lady. All my husbands have been like that, and none of them more so than Jimmy Livesey. I know he's an actor, and I swore that I would never marry another actor, not after the last one, but Jimmy's different. He's a force of nature. I mean, he's hardly an actor at all.

This didn't surprise Paul, who was familiar enough with the Livesey oeuvre to know that he wasn't an actor in any conventional sense of the word as, whatever role he played, he was always just Jimmy Livesey in a different hat. Since leaving *New Town* he had starred in one short-lived vehicle after another, playing a policeman, a security guard, a soldier, a hitman and, most implausibly, a 'maverick investigative journalist'. You could only tell which by the costume.

As the subject of Jimmy Livesey, the current 'Mr Eileen Weathers', had come up, Paul decided to do a little investigative journalism of his own.

Paul: How would you describe your relationship with Jimmy? The papers are always full of stories about how 'tempestuous' it is.

Eileen: You don't want to believe everything you read in the papers.

Paul: But what about that recent claim that he'd hit you? There were pictures of you with a black eye.

Eileen: And as I said to journalists at the time, darlin', I walked into a cupboard door.

Paul: Is that true? I mean, if we're going to work on this book together it's important to know you're telling me the truth.

Eileen: (*after a long pause*) All right, Paul. I can see that this is going to be harder than I thought. No, it's OK, I'll tell you the truth, the whole truth and nothing but the truth, but you're going to have to be kind to me. I'm a very honest person, darlin', and I don't like lying, but sometimes you have to hold things back just to protect yourself.

Paul: We can always take stuff out at a later date if you think it's too…

Eileen: The truth is that my marriage isn't a bed of roses. Jimmy is… well, Jimmy is a good-looking young man with a lot of time on his hands. I work very hard, as you know, and when I'm not at *New Town* I've got all my charity commitments. What I look for in a husband is a tower of strength. Someone I can come home to at the end of another day of being Eileen Weathers, and just collapse into his arms. Someone who will support me and understand my weaknesses…Not someone who sees every single day as some kind of competition.

Paul: And is that what Jimmy does?

Eileen: Christ, darlin', you have no idea. Look, this isn't for public consumption, but I've got to tell someone, and I already feel that I can trust you…

Paul: (*glowing with pride*) Thank you.

Eileen: Well, to be honest, Jimmy hasn't been the husband that I hoped he'd be. He's always running around doing his own thing, and I think you know what I mean by that. Please don't ask me to go into details, it's just too painful. And when I come home for a bit of TLC, he's either not here or he's pissed and in a foul mood and he takes it all out on me.

Paul: You mean he hits you?

Eileen: Oh, that. No, that really was an accident. He's not a wife-beater. He was drunk and he lashed out and I happened to be in the way, but the papers are never going to understand that, are they? Hence the little white lie. I could flatten him if I wanted to. That's one of the good things about growing up with south London gangsters, darlin'. I know how to take care of myself. But the truth of the matter is that Jimmy goes his own way and I go mine.

Paul: It wasn't always that way, though, was it?

Eileen: No, it was good enough to start off with. I mean, he was this gorgeous young stud and I was the big star, and we spent the first year…well, pardon my French, darlin', and I'm sure you'll find a delicate way of putting this, but we spent the first year fucking each other's brains out. Couldn't get enough of each other. He was married at the time – so was I, for that matter – so we had to keep it all hush-hush. As soon as we went official, the fun went out of it. So here we are, Mr and Mrs James Livesey in name only. Look, if you don't mind, I'll take a little break now. Turn your whatsit off, darlin', and let's have a drink.

Over a sherry, Paul brought the conversation round – brilliantly, he thought – to matters more contentious.

'Well,' he said, sipping daintily, 'thank you for being so honest.'

'I owe that much to the fans.'

'I think the fans love you because of all the rumours rather than despite them.'

'The real fans just want me to be happy.'

'I don't know,' said Paul, mustering his courage. 'I think lots of people regard you as an icon…'

'I'm a very normal woman, Paul,' said Eileen with a steely gaze. Paul could see the shutters coming down.

'But those rumours make you fascinating.'

'What rumours would those be, darlin'?'

'Well, I mean, lots of people have said over the years that, er…'

'OK.' Eileen put her drink down carefully on a little occasional table. 'Turn your bloody thing back on, because I'm only going to say this once and I don't want any confusion on the matter. Go on. I mean it.'

The red light on Paul's tape recorder winked on.

Eileen: I know perfectly well what you're talking about, so I won't beat about the bush. You mean these silly bloody stories that I'm a – what? – a transvestite.

Paul: (*meekly*) A transsexual…

Eileen: A transsexual. A trans-fucking-sexual. I mean, Christ, Paul, look at me. Do I look like a man? Do I look like a fucking drag queen?

Paul: (*lying*) Of course not, but…

Eileen: I'm a woman. What more can I say? Short of dropping my drawers and showing everyone my mary-jane…

Paul: So where did these stories come from? Maybe that's what we should address…

Eileen: They're stupid bloody lies that someone made up to hurt me.

Paul: But if they're just lies, how come they're so persistent?

Eileen: (*pause*) OK, darlin'. (*sighs*) Let's deal with this now. I'm sorry I got angry…It just hurts me every time it comes up.

Paul: I can understand that…

Eileen: Don't get me wrong. I've got nothing against transie-whatsits, and I love drag queens. I used to know Danny La Rue back in the '60s, of course, and I've seen some very funny ones doing me at charity events. I support a lot of Aids work, so of course I'm friends with a lot of that type.

Paul: Naturally.

Eileen: The truth of the matter is that it all started as a joke. A silly joke that backfired on me very badly.

Paul: You mean you started the rumours?

Eileen: You could say that. I was having troubles in my first marriage to Charlie Weathers – that's a whole different story, of course. But the thing that the papers wouldn't leave alone was that I had never provided him with a child. He'd gone around telling everyone at the time of our marriage how much he was looking forward to having a family, and I went along with it. But for some reason I never conceived. Not for want of trying, either. He wasn't a young man, even then, but, God, he was a randy old sod! And I was gorgeous, of course, still only in my twenties, very glamorous, and they all expected me to start popping kids out left, right and centre. But I couldn't.

Paul: Couldn't? You mean there was a problem?

Eileen: There was a problem somewhere, darlin', that's all I'm saying.

Paul: So it was Charlie who was…infertile.

Eileen: That's a hard thing for any man to accept.

Paul: And the papers assumed it was you.

Eileen: Oh, they said hurtful things, darlin'. They said I was selfish for putting my career before having a family; it's hard to believe now, but this was in the '70s, and feminism still had a long way to go. I like to think that I helped it along a little bit.

Paul: So what happened?

Eileen: In the end I got so fed up with them digging their noses into our private lives that I made up a story, more a joke than anything else, that I was really a boy, and that's why I couldn't have children. I thought they'd take it in the spirit it was said, a throwaway remark, and just leave us to get on with our lives. But they didn't. They wouldn't come out and print the story, not back then – that sort of thing was considered beyond the pale in them days. But they started hinting. They'd say things about how big my feet were, or how my voice was 'gruff'. They started captioning photos with things like 'Oh, boy! It's Eileen Weathers!' And there was always some silly queen who said he knew me in the old days, when bla bla bla.

Paul: Why didn't you just come out publicly and deny it?

Eileen: I may be stupid, darlin', but I'm not mad. You learn one thing very quickly in my business, and that's never to take on the press at their own game. If I'd stood up and made a statement, it would have made front-page news rather than just some silly little story on page seven. Even if the headline was 'Eileen Weathers is NOT a Man', people would have thought there was no smoke without fire. So I let it lie. People see what they want to see, don't they, darlin'? If it gives them a giggle to think that I'm some kind of circus freak, there's no great harm done, is there? I'm well past the age where that sort of thing worries me.

It was only later, when Paul was flicking through his rapidly expanding cuttings file, that two things sprang to his attention.

Firstly, that Charlie Weathers became a father later in life, after his marriage to Eileen had been dissolved and he was dating a younger actress. Secondly, the Weathers-trannie rumours dated from a much earlier period; even in 1973, five years before her wedding, the up-and-coming TV showgirl was the subject of hints about her 'exotic past' and, indeed, some catty remarks about the size of her feet. And there were the photographs – old and grainy, but clear enough – of showgirl Kiki de Londres, travesty toast of Soho and Pigalle. Was it – could it be – a young Eileen?

The interviews took four hours, after which Eileen looked tired and fragile and, Paul thought, older than when she opened the door. It made him like her more. He had come expecting an armour-plated dragon, and he had found something much more to his taste. She was mercurial, insecure, vulnerable but, on the whole, he felt, genuine. When he clicked his tape recorder off for the last time, conscious of the lateness of the hour and the volume of material, Eileen rubbed her eyes and sighed deeply.

'I'm tired, I'm hungry and I'm gagging for a drink,' she said.

'I'll leave you to it. Thank you so much.'

'Oh, do you have to rush? Won't you stay for a bite to eat?'

'I wouldn't want to intrude…' Paul looked at his watch.

'I'm sorry!' said Eileen, suddenly flustered. 'You've got someone to rush home to, of course. How selfish of me.'

'No, not at all. There's nobody waiting for me.'

Eileen looked at him for a moment – appraisingly, it seemed to Paul.

'I'm sure Danny can whip up something tasty.'

The thought of Danny whipping anything at all was enough to clinch the deal. 'Well, if you're sure.'

'Dan-neeeee!' shouted Eileen in the voice that had so often echoed across the *New Town* lot. 'We're starving to death in here. You're not veggie or anything ghastly like that, are you?'

Supper was the kind of informal affair that Paul dreamed of, with the best of everything dished up as if it was just any old crap from Tesco. Danny poured drinks, and occasionally perched on a piece of furniture to stuff food into his mouth. His manners were positively Neanderthal, which stimulated Paul's salivary glands even more than the cheese, wine and pâté.

Eileen, meanwhile, was charm personified. She flattered, but so subtly that Paul didn't realise. She asked him questions about his personal and professional life, subjects on which he was not usually willing to be drawn but which he now found himself describing in voluminous detail. He spoke of his struggles to complete his second novel, as if it was just a matter of time before the final full stop. He portrayed himself as a rakehell and a heartbreaker, at least when Danny wasn't in the room; when he was there, Paul just concentrated on looking extremely available. Within thirty minutes he'd revealed more about himself than Eileen had managed in four hours.

'Have you ever had your heart broken, Paul?' She regarded him over the top of a crystal goblet, freshly filled with something cold and white. ('It's a rather nice Pouilly,' said Danny, massacring the French adorably.)

'Oh, yes…' said Paul, looking down into his napkin. 'More than once.'

'I felt that as soon as you walked through the door,' said Eileen, wildly improvising. 'I could never open myself up to someone who hasn't…suffered.'

'I've had my fair share,' said Paul, conscious of the fact that Danny was hovering, a fragile crystal goblet grasped in one huge, simian paw. 'Hasn't everyone?'

'Danny's never had his heart broken, have you, lover boy?'

'Naaaah.' Danny grinned, drained his glass and stood up. 'Is that all, modom? I've got work to do.'

'Yes, run along and let us talk.'

'You stayin', cock? Or what?'

'No…' said Paul. 'I must get home…'

'Carriages in an hour, Danny. That will do.' She dismissed him with a wave of the famous manicure. 'I hope you won't think I'm some sad old has-been, darlin'.'

'Why on earth would I think that?'

'All this talk about the past, I suppose. Makes you melancholy.' She stood up, glass in hand, and drifted to the open French window. The pool lights played around the patio. She stared out, lost in thought.

'The past…Wouldn't life be easier if you could just wave a wand and make it disappear? If you could right the wrongs, take away the hurt, make it like something out of a storybook?'

'That would be nice.' Paul wondered what she was getting at.

'But you can't, can you? The past is what we are. We can't control it and we can't change it.'

'But we can present it in such a way…'

'Yes, that's true. But I don't want this to be another load of old showbiz waffle. That's why it's so important that I've got you, Paul. I feel that already. The people at Six don't really understand me. They threw me in at the deep end – just me and my past – and left me to struggle. But there's so much, Paul. So much has happened. I can't face it all alone.'

'You're not alone any more,' said Paul, gulping with emotion. 'I'm here now.'

chapter four

Each car that pulled into the drive of the Liveseys' Essex mansion was longer than the last. From eight o'clock they'd been arriving, only half an hour after the last caterer's truck had disappeared (they'd be back in the morning to collect the debris). Last to leave had been the florist, a man so deeply mired in cocaine abuse that it had taken him all day to arrange the vast banks of white lilies that lined the entrance hall. Finally, Danny had to convince him that he was not a guest, and he departed, snorting and snuffling, his clothes streaked with pollen and powder.

Eileen was fixing a silk lily into her hair, specially up for the occasion. 'It's not my man's birthday every day,' she told Lorraine, the *New Town* hair and make-up girl who had become her personal stylist for the evening. 'Every bloody bastard in the business is going to be here for a sniff round. Try and make me look halfway decent.'

Lorraine narrowed her eyes and peered through a stinging haze of cannabis smoke. 'Calm down, babe. You'll be the belle of the ball.'

'I wish my husband would tell me things like that,' said Eileen.

'Oh, shut up and pass me the drugs,' said Jimmy, who was getting ready on the other side of what they quaintly called their dressing room. 'You look fine…for a woman of your age.'

'Christ, Livesey, you're a cunt,' said Eileen. 'You can roll your own fucking joint.'

'That's nice, on my birthday.'

'Don't kid yourself, my dear. Kid everyone else, by all means, if you think that a pretence of being happily married will get you a job, but not yourself.'

'You are a mean-spirited old hag.'

'Less of the "old" my sweet, if you don't mind.'

This sub-Strindbergian badinage had been going on for the last hour, since Danny had brought Jimmy home, half cut after a long lunch with 'friends'. He resented everything – the effort to which Eileen had gone to rally the great and the good, the expense (hers) lavished on catering and decoration, the willingness to put on a united front to the profession. And it was all with one object in view: to get Jimmy a job. This, Eileen rightly believed, was the only hope of saving her marriage, and she was willing to give it one last try. An idle Jimmy was a bad Jimmy, chasing tail, drinking and gambling money that wasn't his to waste. At least if he was employed he would be too busy, and too tired, to create the kind of scenes that were becoming so regular a feature of their married life. Falling over in public was the least of it; it was the tactlessness of his infidelities that irked Eileen. Attending openings and awards with his bits of totty, for instance, or setting himself up for yet another kiss and tell. It amazed Eileen that there were still newspaper editors willing to pay these scrubbers for stories on Jimmy Livesey, who, as well she knew, was all but finished as an actor. His only selling point in news terms was the fact that he was, to his constant annoyance, Mr Eileen Weathers. A story about him was in reality a story about her. An invitation to him – usually to something that only the desperate would attend – was an admission that they couldn't get her. All of this confirmed Eileen's star status, but it wasn't doing a lot for her home life.

She handed the joint back to Lorraine and started to feel calmer.

'Shut your eyes, babe,' said Lorraine. 'Finishing touches.' She dabbed around the eyes with a tiny glitter pen.

'Oh, for God's sake, Lorraine,' said Jimmy, knocking back a whisky, 'don't make her look like a fucking drag queen.'

In the main reception room, a huge hollow cube swathed for the occasion with white silk, the early guests were assembling. They represented the lower end of the pecking order, and didn't care who knew it – the neighbours, relatives and employees who were there to enjoy themselves and not to work. Among them was Paul Mackrell, unpartnered and seemingly unable to engage in conversation with his fellow guests. He was always like this at parties: a wallflower, a fly on the wall, flattering himself that, as a writer, it was his duty to observe rather than to participate. He sipped a glass of champagne, wondering if he could capture the rich detail of the evening in the style of Emile Zola.

From his position by the buffet, he could see the front door where Danny, dressed in something resembling a footman's uniform, was meeting and greeting in lieu of his employers. Danny had given Paul a particularly warm handshake on his arrival and had muttered something along the lines of 'I'll catch you later, cock'. Since first they met all those weeks ago, through long evenings of interviews and intimate suppers, Paul had convinced himself that Danny felt for him something of what he felt for Danny, in other words lust. Whether or not this was true he intended to find out.

It was nearly nine when Eileen descended the broad hardwood staircase on Jimmy's arm. Paul watched them as they worked the vestibule, never quite together but never far apart, as if connected by an invisible cord of love. They smiled, they joked, they laughed and occasionally Eileen would whisper in her husband's ear. He deferred to her, recharged her glass, hovered when necessary. Perhaps, thought Paul, he wasn't such a bad actor after all.

The second wave was arriving now – those with some status in the profession, those who might reasonably regard themselves as Eileen and Jimmy's peers. They were the producers, the writers, the commissioning editors, the heads of this and the controllers of that, who might be able to give Jimmy a job. This was never openly mentioned, but it was so obviously the point of the party that it might as well have been printed on the invitations. 'Join us at home to celebrate Jimmy's thirty-fifth birthday. Please bring a contract.'

Here was a gaggle of Eileen's *New Town* co-stars. Leah Wilkinson, the 'troubled' (translation: drug-addled) young actress who played her daughter Mandy, more often suspended from the show than not…Tim Boreham, who had played Dr David Ditchling both man and boy and who was now so institutionalised that he could talk nothing but shop (the crew called him 'Tim Bore'em-to-Death')…Terence Lee, who, on screen, was all fruity correctness as Dr Lazarus but preferred to relax off-duty in a capacious muumuu, gold pumps and just a hint of blusher…T. J. Daniels and his nineteen-year-old girlfriend, who headed straight for the bar and were soon under it…Tyrone, Gemma and Steve, the *New Town* bratpack, who worshipped the ground Eileen walked on and hoped, one day, to have their own Essex mansions. Eileen kissed them all, Jimmy shook them forcefully by the hand. 'Still slaving away at the factory, Tim?' he said to his former co-star. 'You want to get out of there, mate. Develop a bit of range. Best thing I ever did…'

They smiled and returned kisses, then moved through to the reception room to discuss it all.

'Range!' sniffed Tim Boreham. 'The only range he's got is in that posh fitted kitchen.'

Paul, strategically obscured by a floral arrangement, heard every word and couldn't wait to relay it to his ever-widening circle of friends.

'Pay him no mind,' said Terence, who preferred to be called 'Terri' when he was 'in mufti'. 'He hasn't worked since that awful travesty he did for ITV. What was it called?'

'*From Our Own Reporter*,' said Leah, who had an awful lot of time on her hands in which to watch TV.

'Oh, that was good,' said Tyrone, who looked up to Jimmy (he was only fifteen, poor lamb). 'He was cool in it.'

'My dear,' said Terri, draping an arm around Tyrone's shoulder (he did this often), 'neither was it good, nor he cool, but an abomi-NA-tion!' Terri, who had been acting all his life, was not a great fan of modern television. 'A pot-pourri of second-hand tat. Listen and learn. Oooh, champagne.' With practised ease, he replaced his empty glass with a full one. 'Down the little red road it goes. Here's how.'

'Where's Marjorie?' asked Gemma.

'How should I know?' snapped Terri, who had little time for the female members of the cast. 'She's only my screen wife, you know.'

'Marjorie wouldn't come here if you paid her,' said Tim, a reliable archivist of all the green-room gossip. 'Don't forget what Jimmy called her that night at the Baftas. A dried-up old prune. She told me she'd never darken his door again.'

'My dear child,' said Terri, for whom Tim, now forty, would always be a child, 'that was over ten years ago.'

'Well, that's what she said, that's all.'

'Oh, Timothy, you are a tedious little boy. Now, Steve,' said Terri, turning to his current protégé, the dumb hunk who played Gemma's screen husband, 'why don't I take you for a little tour of inspection. Perhaps you'd care to swim, hmm?' And, grabbing Steve by the arm, he swished from the room, leaving only the scent of vetiver behind him. Terri, who had friends in low places, was already familiar with Steve's ill-advised 'physique modelling' past, and was eager to see the goods at first hand.

'Well, I liked it,' said Tyrone, still smarting from the attack on Jimmy. 'I wouldn't mind a job like that.'

'Maybe, when you grow up,' said Gemma, a hard-faced piece of work with her hair scraped back from her forehead. 'I'm going to find Jimmy. He and I've got projects to discuss.'

From the rear, observed Paul, it was plain to see that she was wearing no knickers.

'What's up with her?' sulked Tyrone.

'The host, if she gets her way,' said Leah. 'Slut.' She spoke, needless to say, as one who had humped the host herself for a short while.

Tyrone was disappointed; he'd hoped to get off with Gemma tonight. But then he noticed a girl nearer his own age – the daughter of a neighbour – eyeballing him from across the room. 'He shoots, he scores,' he muttered and swaggered off in character as Dean, *New Town*'s teen tearaway.

'Well, that just leaves you and—' began Tim, but Leah, knowing only too well that if she didn't make a hasty escape she would be Bore'emed-to-Death, had dematerialised.

There was a hubbub from the hallway, a crescendo of delighted squawks – Damian Davies had arrived. As the only *New Town* alumnus to have made good, his appearance at any function was greeted as a message of hope from the outside world. Tim, who considered Damian to be 'a good mate' even though they had not spoken since Davies left the show, ambled off to join the crowd. Paul drifted after him, to feast his eyes on the actor consistently voted 'Sexiest Man on Television'. In the flesh, he did not disappoint.

Eileen was in the front rank.

'Ah, my little boy!' she said, kissing Damian on a chiselled jaw. 'You've come to see your old mum.'

'Wouldn't miss this for the world, Eileen. You know Gavin, don't you?'

He gestured to a handsome middle-aged man at his side.

'Gavin Graham. Well, fuck me. You've got a nerve.'

'I certainly have. Nice to see you, Eileen.'

'I wonder – shall I have you thrown out now, or later?' Danny hovered muscularly behind her.

'I haven't come to fight, Eileen. Just doing a little business.'

'Gavin represents me now,' said Damian.

'Then your career must be in trouble,' said Eileen.

'And I'd very much like to represent you too,' said Gavin, unflustered.

'Jimmy and me?'

'Don't make me laugh, darling,' said Gavin, feigning a kiss. 'I don't work with losers. It's you I'm after.'

'Mwah, mwah,' went Eileen, kissing the air but acutely aware of Gavin's handsome tanned face, faintly redolent of Old Spice, next to hers. 'Go away and drink my liquor, you snake.'

'Later, gorgeous.'

Even Paul Mackrell, from the height of his ivory tower, had some inkling of Gavin Graham's reputation. He was the publicist who was more famous than his clients. In the Faustian universe of twenty-first-century show business, he was Mephistopheles. He promised wealth, fame and sex, and he delivered. And when they came whining to him about loss of privacy, about personal lives shattered and loved ones doorstepped, he reminded them that fame comes with a price tag. He told them so at the start – it was his standard line at the initial lunch – and he watched with relish as, every time, they ignored his warnings. Everywhere he went – and he went everywhere – he left behind him a whiff of sulphur.

Eileen Weathers had particular reason to dislike Gavin Graham. It was he who placed the most damaging stories about her, who kept alive the monstrous lies from her past, who lined up a string of kiss-and-tell tarts for Jimmy to stumble on. Eileen was too wise to imagine that Gavin had any personal animus towards her; she knew that he was just a clever man doing his job very well. In fact, despite the froideur of her greeting, she was secretly pleased to see him. The grapevine knew that Gavin had been after Eileen's business for some time, and it was only his continued persecution of Jimmy that prevented her from signing. Gavin, it was known, could make even the brightest star shine a little brighter. Given the parlous state of *New Town* and her own imminent launch into the world of publishing, Eileen could use his brand of snake oil. She had even mentioned this to her husband, who said in no uncertain terms that if she went 'anywhere near that piece of shit' he would…well, you get the picture.

Now her prime concern was in preventing Jimmy from punching Gavin's lights out in front of the assembled guests, among whom was nearly everyone who could get his career back on track. Punching Gavin Graham was a very bad career move, as any number of unemployed actors and footballers could testify from the dole queue.

Eileen grasped the nettle.

'Did you see who's here, my sweet?' she whispered in Jimmy's ear. He prised himself away from Gemma Leeds, who had suctioned herself on to his face.

'Nah. Who?'

'Probably doesn't matter, as you're making a good job of throwing this opportunity down the drain without his assistance, but Gavin Graham has just arrived.'

'Gavin GRAHAM!' squealed Gemma, scuttling off to meet him.

'That piece of…'

'Yes, darlin', that incredibly powerful and influential publicist, you're absolutely right. Now, isn't it kind of him to come to your birthday party?'

'Who invited him? You stupid…'

'What's that? "How nice of such an important person to want to help us out"?'

'Whaddya mean,' said Jimmy, wiping lipstick from his face and sourly eyeballing Gavin across the hall, where Gemma gibbered and quivered beside him.

'He says he's interested in representing…us.'

'He can sling his hook.'

'My precious husband,' said Eileen, laying an affectionate hand on Jimmy's arm (people were looking). 'In your position, I'd be desperately grateful for any hooks that came my way. Now, go and nibble.' She looked over at Gavin and the frenetically pouting Gemma. 'Before some other trout does.'

Wherever there are actors, there will be journalists, and a chosen few (those who had written nice things in the last year) had been invited. Eileen remembered none of them, but kissed them and called them 'darlin', which was her job at these functions.

When she was out of earshot, they gathered by the bar, as journalists will.

'So it's true, then,' said one, who worked for a newspaper.

'What?' said the editor of a TV listings magazine.

'About Tracey Reynolds.'

'Who?' said a freelance features writer, who was so out of the loop that he didn't even recognise the *New Town* producer's name.

'Sacked.'

'No!'

'Where is she, then?'

'Just because she's not here doesn't mean she's been…'

'No? Well, that's not what Terri told me.'

'Terry? Terry who?'

'Terri Lee. He's…well, he's a good mate of mine.'

This meant that the journalist had recently got drunk at a party and allowed Terri Lee to fumble in his lap.

'And what did Terri tell you?'

'Gone. Kaput. Adios. History.'

'Well, of course there are rumours…'

'And she's not here.'

'Nor are any number of people.'

'Not what Terri told me…Hey! Hi! Terri! Mate!'

Terri, in a rather damp muumuu, had just walked back in from the patio, where he was watching Steve Seddon ploughing up and down the pool. He only wanted to grab a bottle and go.

'What? Who are you?'

'You remember, Terri. National Telly Awards last week. Great night.'

'I have no idea what you're talking about. Excuse me.' He waddled off, clutching champagne.

'Your sources,' gloated the rival, 'are impeccable.'

But, in fact, the rumours were right: Tracey Reynolds was no longer *New Town*'s producer. In the weeks since we met her, fumbling her way through a script conference, she had faced open mutiny from her staff, who, sensing weakness, turned on her like rats in a cage. Tracey, unable to defend herself and without support from her superiors, rolled over without much of a struggle. When the call finally came from Nick Needs's PA inviting her for lunch, she accepted her destiny with relief. Now she could go back to that raft of exciting documentary features that she was preparing for the independent sector.

The announcement had not yet been made, but the people who mattered already knew. Gavin Graham knew – and that explained, in part, his presence at the party. With the show in trouble, the time was ripe to press his suit to Eileen. He wanted her to leave the show, generate a frenzy of media interest and then launch big in a new tailor-made vehicle that would bleed dry the last few years of her working life.

Eileen knew – and she was not sorry to see Tracey go, although she had nothing against her personally. She was just another in the long line of *New Town* producers who had been chewed up and spat back to obscurity.

Terri Lee knew – but then he knew everything, and if he didn't he was willing to make it up.

The rest of the cast would learn when they opened tomorrow's papers – those who could read, at least.

Paul had spent so long by the bar that he was now thinking less of Emile Zola and more of Danny the minder. He found him in the kitchen, overseeing an army of caterers.

'Garnish, garnish!' growled Danny at a tiny woman who was about to hand round a tray of canapés devoid of leaves, lemon slices or radish roses. With a flick of the wrist, Danny scattered decorative veg and pushed the waitress through the door. He saw Paul lurking in the passage.

'Paolo! Come in 'ere and give me a hand!'

These were the words Paul had longed to hear, minus the final 'job'.

He dodged canapés and joined Danny at the brushed-steel work surface.

'All right, mate? You look smart!' He ruffled Paul's hair. Paul nearly went face down into the sink.

'What can I…do for you?'

'Pour me a fuckin' drink for starters. I've got a stash of decent stuff under the sink.'

Paul bent over and discovered an unopened bottle of Dom Pérignon, which was certainly a step up from the Perrier-Jouët served to guests. He fumbled with the foil and the wire cage.

'Oh, hand it over,' said Danny, and within seconds his huge hands wrested the cork from the bottle's mouth. Foam bulged at the rim, then ran in a white stream down the side. Danny licked it off and handed the wet bottle to Paul.

'Dish it out, mate,' he said. 'Oops, there goes a vol-au-vent.' He bent over to rescue the little mass of crust and slime, then stood up, red in the face, and put it back on the tray. 'That lot won't know the difference. Our little secret, Paolo.'

This was all proving too much for Paul, whose instincts told him to flee. 'I'll go and mingle…'

'Hold yer horses,' said Danny. 'You don't want to talk to that load of old poofs. Stay here and keep me company.'

'Well, if I'm not in the way…'

'If you get in the way, I'll just have to squeeze past,' said Danny, winking and sticking a vol-au-vent into Paul's open mouth. It sat on his tongue, unchewed, for a full five seconds.

While Paul was out of the way, the party was heating up. Nick Needs, head of drama at Channel Six, had arrived, and after an orgy of bowing and scraping from the assembled minions he cornered Eileen in her 'yoga room' – a completely functionless chamber that the last interior decorator had painted in a cacophony of yellows and golds. The cocaine florist had added his own touch with a vast arrangement of sulphur roses.

'Thanks for coming, Nick.'

'My pleasure.'

'We don't see much of you on the lot these days.'

'You will from now on.'

'That sounds ominous, darlin''

'You've got nothing to worry about, Eileen.'

'So when are we getting a new boss to replace…what was her name?'

'Soon enough. You'll be the first to know.'

'I should hope so.'

'In the meantime, if there's anything you need to discuss, you only have to call my PA.'

'Now why would I want to do that,' said Eileen, who could stun bigger men than Nick Needs with a little focused flirtation, 'when I have you here in the flesh all to myself?'

'What's on your mind?'

'Well,' said Eileen, pacing about the golden carpet, 'there is the small matter of…my darlin' husband.'

'Ah. How is Jimmy?'

'You tell me, Nick.'

'I don't follow.'

'I married a successful young actor. I seem to have ended up with some kind of pariah. Just wondering if you could shed any light.'

'Eileen,' said Nick, who believed in speaking his mind. 'A word to the wise.

Jimmy's free to look elsewhere. He knows that. We're not actively developing projects for him.'

'Couldn't you see your way clear to developing the tiniest little project, as a favour?'

'No.'

'You can't blame a girl for trying…' said Eileen, stepping close to Nick and brushing an imaginary piece of fluff from his lapel. 'We've been friends for a long time…'

'Must I put it more clearly?'

'I'm afraid you're about to.'

'Jimmy won't work for Channel Six again while I'm head of drama. He's cost us too much money. He's not up to it, Eileen. You know that as well as I do.'

'But the public, Nick…' Eileen wasn't going to give up without a struggle; she knew her husband couldn't act his way out of a paper bag, but she longed for a quiet life. 'The public love him. They recognise him in the street – more than me, to tell the truth. I ought to be jealous. He gets mountains of fan mail.'

'I'm sorry. We can't risk our reputation on another underperforming star vehicle. We're focusing our energies on developing new talent.'

'And I suppose that means that the old faithfuls who made you a rich man can go fuck 'emselves.' She tossed her head and glared at him. The stamens on her artificial lily quivered.

'Your position is safe, Eileen. Your husband is a free agent. That's all I can say.'

'Oh, well. That's that, then. Run along, darlin'. I have other guests to attend to.'

It was at this point that Eileen Weathers realised her marriage was on the rocks, although you'd never have known it as she emerged from the yoga room, wreathed in smiles, champagne in hand, a golden glow behind her. She greeted guests, exchanged small talk and laughed her raucous launderette laugh. But her mind was elsewhere, calculating the cost, financial and personal, of a divorce. She wondered how she might tactfully come to terms with Gavin Graham before the night was through; he, if anyone, could turn personal loss into publicity profit.

Divorce, like so many intimate acts, hurts less the more you do it. When Eileen split up with her first proper boyfriend, she cried for a week, but then again she was only twelve. Her first legal husband, Charlie Weathers, parted company like a gentleman, which, despite it all, he was. Her second husband, Brian the builder, left when he was told to, with that permanently baffled expression that he'd worn throughout their marriage. She'd got the Essex mansion out of that one, which eased the pain considerably.

Jimmy was a harder nut to crack. The *Daily Herald* would take his side, and if she didn't secure the services of Gavin Graham she'd have all the big guns against her. But she had a few tricks up her sleeve: the black eye (yes, she had photographed it), the endless kiss and tells, the drinking, the abuse…

It would have surprised her guests to know that she was plotting the divorce even as she flitted around her husband, who by now had abandoned Gemma Leeds and was showing more interest than was strictly necessary in one of the transvestite hostesses who had been hired in a job lot from a West End club. Would he never learn?

Eileen looked back with bitterness but not anger at her five-year marriage, and we may as well join her, as the opportunity may not arise again.

It had all begun much more than five years ago, as early as 1991 when Jimmy, then just twenty-one and fresh from the building site on which he had been discovered, had so sensationally joined the cast of *New Town*. He was a complete unknown, as unactorish an actor as you could ever hope to meet (unfortunately, this extended to his lack of talent). Eileen wasn't the only one who had fallen for him: Terri was all abuzz in the early days, as were a very large percentage of *New Town*'s viewers, who made him an instant pin-up and were prepared to overlook his shortcomings as long as he took his shirt off a lot. He did this on screen, and, crucially, he did it when he visited Eileen's dressing room to 'run over his lines'. They became lovers there and then, on her shabby old couch.

That couch saw a lot of between-takes action over the coming months, and soon Eileen and Jimmy's affair was the talk of the lot. *New Town*'s publicists struggled to keep it under wraps, but when the on-screen chemistry between the handsome handyman and the mature laundress began to capture the public imagination, they switched tactics and began to hint to anyone who'd listen that this was a 'real-life' love match. Storylines were changed in order to engineer an affair between the two, while Eileen and Jimmy's spouses could do nothing but fume impotently in empty homes. Eileen was, at the time, Mrs Brian Champion in private life – and her builder husband was erecting their Essex love nest in good faith. Jimmy had unwisely wed his childhood sweetheart, an inoffensive hairdresser whose wildest dreams went no further than her own salon. She was ditched without a second thought. (Worry not: she made enough from selling her story to realise her salon dreams.)

Public sympathy stayed with the guilty lovers for as long as Eileen remained in *New Town*. But when she took a well-earned two-year break, the tide turned. People suddenly remembered the age difference. They remembered (or were reminded) that Eileen had a string of broken marriages in her wake – her own, and those of her various spouses, nearly all of whom had left wives and children to be with her. Every bit of dirt was dug, particularly on Jimmy, who hadn't been too fussy about where he sowed his wild oats. A string of sweethearts came forward, brandishing little bundles who they claimed were his – and it was possible, for Jimmy was excessively fertile. And then, of course, it was pointed out yet again that Eileen alone of all his conquests had failed to provide an heir. The fact that, by the time of their marriage in 2000, she was very much menopausal, did nothing to silence the wagging tongues. The old rumours surfaced once more, those same smudgy pictures of Kiki de Londres, the toast of Soho and Pigalle, those 'former friends' who knew 'her' as a boy…

Undeterred, Eileen and Jimmy wed – and the sparkle faded from the romance. Jimmy announced that he was leaving *New Town* to pursue several interesting offers from Hollywood – which amounted to little more than sitting by a pool for three months getting drugs and blow jobs off starlets. At least one of these was an employee of Gavin Graham, whose influence extended to the scuzzier end of Hollywood Boulevard, and no sooner had the plastic-breasted lovely wiped her mouth than she was on the phone to the arch publicist. Kiss and tell isn't the behaviour of a lady – but this was no lady. She was still officially a he, and had been thrown in Jimmy's path simply to see if he would bite and, if he bit, whether he would go on to chew. Jimmy, who wasn't fussy, bit and chewed and even swallowed.

For the last five years, Jimmy and Eileen had tolerated each other. He needed her money, her status and her contacts, even if, since the Hollywood débâcle, he had flaunted his infidelities in her face. She needed an athletic young stud at her side, even if that athletic young stud was rapidly turning into a middle-aged has-been.

All of this was going through Eileen's mind as she framed herself in the kitchen doorway.

'I hate to interrupt you young lovebirds,' she said as Danny was pouring the umpteenth glass of Dom Pérignon, 'but I need to borrow you for a moment. If you can spare him, Paul?'

'Course he can,' said Danny, cantering across the kitchen floor to his boss's side.

'I won't keep him long, darlin',' said Eileen. Paul buried his nose in the bubbles.

'Go and mingle, Paolo. I'll find you later.'

Danny trotted after his mistress like a faithful pet, and Paul found himself wondering, not for the first time, if Danny was more than just a minder. He drifted through the party, none too steady on his feet, and out to the patio, where Terri Lee was towelling down Steve Seddon.

'This little piggy had roast beef, the lucky queen, and this little piggy had none. Don't wriggle so. It's important to dry between the toes. There's a good boy.'

Paul settled into a poolside lounger and closed his eyes. Perhaps it was the champagne, perhaps it was the gentle lapping of blue waters, but whatever the cause he nodded off.

When he awoke, it was to the sound of screaming.

chapter five

Paul's mouth and eyes were dry, his head fuzzy and he had no idea how long he had been asleep. The pool lights had been switched off, and he realised, on waking, that he was shivering with cold.

The scream – if it had not been part of a drunken dream – came from nearby. He sat up on the lounger, took off his glasses and rubbed his eyes. There were muffled voices, footsteps and the slam of a door.

Paul got to his feet, and as he did so a figure materialised in the French doors.

'There you are, mate! Been looking for you all evening!'

It was Danny, and he was out of breath.

'What was that scream?'

'Oh, nothing. Just the old girl having the usual end-of-the-evening row with Jimmy. Nothing for us to worry about.'

'Sounded like someone had been hurt.'

'No, everything's OK.'

'He's not hitting her again, is he?'

'I swear, on my mother's life, Eileen's fine.'

'Perhaps I'd better…'

'Look, Paolo, you're shivering.' Danny put an arm around his shoulders. 'You know what you need, mate? A nice hot shower.'

He led Paul towards the changing rooms at the far side of the pool, and kept him there for the next hour or so.

*

While Paul was discovering new uses for a bottle of shower gel, the party was reaching a dramatic conclusion.

Eileen had kissed the last of the guests goodbye and was wondering where the birthday boy had got to when a giggle and a scuffle from somewhere above gave her a clue. She mounted the broad hardwood staircase wearily – parties took it out of her these days – and waited silently on the landing. The noises were coming, predictably, from the dressing room.

It wasn't the fact that Jimmy was getting head off another young actress that upset Eileen so much – nor yet that the actress in question was one of her own *New Town* colleagues. She expected no better from Jimmy nor, frankly, from Gemma, whose frosted lipstick was now smeared all over his groin. It wasn't even the fact that Jimmy had flaunted his infidelity in front of everyone who mattered in the business. No – it was something much more threatening than that.

Gemma disengaged her mouth and screamed at the top of her lungs. This was the sound that woke Paul.

Eileen said nothing. She didn't need to; Jimmy started straight into a whining litany of self-justification.

'You couldn't even get one of those bastards to get me a job. You've got no respect for me, and then you have the nerve to complain when I go with someone who does. Well, excuse, me Miss High and Mighty Eileen Bloody Weathers, but I don't need you, and it's about time you bloody well realised it.'

Jimmy had been drinking heavily, and this kind of stuff washed over Eileen. Suddenly, however, her husband seemed to sober up. A sneaky look came into his famously twinkling blue eyes.

'Wouldn't your fans just love to know what a rotten bloody wife you turned out to be? Oh, yes, I could tell them a story or two about what life is really like with Eileen Weathers. Yeah! Maybe I will! Maybe I'll write my own book. What do you thnk of that? I've had offers before now, let me tell you, and if I decided to go to the right editor I could clean up, couldn't I? Yeah, that made you sit up and take notice, you cow. How about it, eh? I'll write my own book. No holds barred. Tell it like it is. Blow your pathetic little bundle of lies out of the water. Eileen Weathers as you've never – and I mean never – seen her before. The truth at last…'

It was at this point that Eileen, drawing deep on her south London roots, delivered a powerful right hook to her husband's no-longer-chiselled jawline. Her rings were like knuckledusters.

Gemma, who had until now remained crumpled on the floor, got to her feet to intervene. This was a mistake, and the force with which Eileen connected with her solar plexus left no doubt that this was, indeed, a south London seamstress's daughter. Gemma staggered from the dressing room, winded and white-faced, slipped at the head of the stairs and plunged down head first. She was saved from certain death by a huge bank of white lilies.

Jimmy knew when it was time to leave. The Porsche's wheels crunched down the drive, gravel flew and Jimmy sped into the night. Eileen knew he was well over the limit, and hoped that a fatal accident might spare her the trouble of a divorce. She closed the front door behind him.

'Hello, what's this?'

Something was groaning under a pile of crushed flowers. Eileen poked it with a toe; it moved and groaned again. Chocolate and Biscuit, the two silky spaniels, came dashing up to sniff and lick at a small pool of blood. From beneath a curtain of hair, a familiar, hard little face appeared.

'Get off, Jimmy…Oh. It's not…'

'No, darlin'. It's another of my dogs. Now get up and get out.'

The pile shifted again, and from it rose what was unmistakably *New Town* starlet Gemma Leeds, still not entirely conscious, bleeding profusely from a cut on her forehead.

'Eileen, I'm so sorry…'

'You should have thought of that before you had sex with my husband, you little scrubber.'

'I didn't…I mean, we never…'

'Oh, I suppose what you were doing doesn't count? Well, it does in my book, darlin', and you've got you-know-what in your hair.'

'God, I hate it when that happens.'

'You'd better leave.'

'I can't…I…' Gemma buckled at the knees and clutched her head. 'I think I'm going to be sick.'

'I don't want two deaths on my conscience, at least not in the same night. You'd better come upstairs.'

Eileen pulled Gemma's arm around her shoulders and half carried her up the broad hardwood staircase – the self-same stairs that, just moments before, she had flung her down. Gemma looked nervous.

'It's all right, darlin'. I'm not going to do it again. Let's get you cleaned up.'

Eileen sat her in front of the bathroom sink and started dabbing away with a cotton wool pad. Gemma burbled. 'I didn't realise that you and Jimmy…I mean, everyone thinks that you and him are like…'

'Have an open relationship? Is that what he tells you? I don't blame you, darlin'. I'd have done the same in your shoes, and to tell you the truth I've done it a million times. But you broke the rule. You know what that is, don't you, darlin'?'

'Don't steal other women's husbands.'

Eileen laughed. 'You're even thicker than you look, sweetheart. Don't get caught.'

Gemma laughed nervously and began to wonder if the evening was going to turn out so badly after all.

'I've got so much to learn,' she said, looking up through wet lashes. 'I've felt so alone since I joined the show. Everyone seems to hate me.'

Eileen wasn't a bad woman; occasionally violent, but not stone-hearted.

'You remind me a lot of myself at your age, darlin'.'

This was exactly what Gemma hoped to hear. 'How did you cope? You must be so strong.'

The worldly-wise survivor was a role Eileen enjoyed playing; it was how she hoped she'd come across in her autobiography.

'We have to work twice as hard as the men,' she said, pouring two brandies from a bottle that she kept in her bedside table. 'We have to look good all the time, we have to be pretty and fragile, and we have to be hard as nails.'

'I'm not sure if I can ever do that, Eileen...' said Gemma convincingly. 'Sometimes I get so lonely.'

She was saying all the right things, and Eileen launched into a monologue about the loneliness of the long-distance diva – hoping she could remember enough for her next session with Paul. She had never had children, as everyone knew, but she started to feel almost maternal to the sodden bundle in her lap.

'...because men are really just little boys, and sometimes you have to spank their bottoms. Take that husband of mine. Oh, I forgot, you already did.'

Gemma burst into fresh tears. 'Oh, Eileen, what have I done?'

'Now then, now then,' said Eileen, dabbing and stroking, 'nothing's broken that can't be mended. You're not the first silly bint I've thrown out of the house, and you won't be the last. Let's have another drink and be friends.'

'I've got so much to learn from you, Eileen.'

Two hours later, when Gemma let herself quietly out of the house as the first birds were singing in the trees, Eileen was fast asleep on the bed, the empty brandy bottle in her hand. Gemma found her little red sports car where she had left it in the drive, put the key into the ignition and drove off, congratulating herself on what she rightly believed to be the greatest performance of her life.

As soon as she got home, she picked up the phone.

'Hello, Gavin Graham? It's Gemma Leeds. You said to phone you if I ever had a good story to sell. Well, how much will I get for this?'

chapter six

There's nothing like a carrot on a stick to stir a writer into action, and in Paul's case the £10,000 carrot was combined with the goad of an impossibly tight deadline. And so, less than a month after his initial meeting with Eileen Weathers, he was delivering the fruits of their collaboration to Six Books.

'Wow, that's amazing!' said Emma, acting editor in Toby's absence. She flicked through forty pages of coherent, error-free prose. 'You've got her birth…gosh… and then her childhood! That's really…I mean…well, great.'

'Perhaps when you've read it you could let me have your feedback, so that I'll have some guidance for the next few chapters.'

Emma blanched. 'I…well, I won't be…I mean, the proofreader will…'

Paul was learning fast that the word 'editor' in a job title didn't necessarily imply any contact with the printed word.

'OK. Who should I talk to about expenses?' This was a subject with which Emma felt more at home.

'I can put those through for you,' she said, beaming. 'Just drop off an invoice with itemised receipts…Oh, you've already done one. Gosh, that much?'

Paul felt confident about bullying young women, and looked at Emma witheringly (he hoped) over the top of his glasses. He mentally put the sum towards a very nice gold ID bracelet he was going to have engraved for Danny.

It was a long time since Paul had showered gifts on a young man, and he intended to make the most of it. After a series of half-hearted affairs with students from the adult education college where he taught, among other things, a course in gay literature, Paul was ready for the real thing. Pale young men with an interest in Alan Hollinghurst were good for a term, or for as long as the student–teacher frisson lasted, but Paul, like the heroes of most of the novels he forced his students to read, was really interested in the unreconstructed bit of rough. Danny, with his number-one crop, his broken nose and his Mediterranean looks, was just the ticket. E. M. Forster would have had a fit of the vapours over him, and he'd have kept Jean Genet busy through nights in solitary confinement.

So in love was Paul that he never stopped to question Danny's motives, preferring to believe – and who wouldn't? – that Dionysian Dan was simply responding to the call of Apollonian Paul.

Needless to say, a steamy-yet-highbrow novel was already being planned along those classical lines.

While Paul found new ways to finance his affair, the powers at Channel Six announced staff and budget cuts on their disastrously underperforming flagship show, *New Town*. A memo came down to Nick Needs – yes, even he had superiors – demanding a decrease in the gap between funding and revenue 'by any means necessary'. As advertisers abandoned the sinking ship like the rats they were, Nick had no choice but to secure his short-term future by laying off as many employees as possible. As for the long term – well, he had plans, as he was about to reveal.

Eileen knew that her future was secure, but the rest of the cast were thrown into an orgy of speculation. The green room began to resemble a DSS waiting area.

'Coach crash,' said Terri Lee, relaxing after a tense scene in which he had been ravished by a proctoscope. 'That's what I've heard. My friend in the script unit told me.' Terri had friends, all of them young and male, in every department from maintenance upwards. 'Half the cast goes on a charabanc to Brighton or somewhere equally ghastly and it goes wildly out of control on the A23, killing the bloody lot of them. It could be any of us, dear,' he added, as colleagues sat around him like disciples. 'But let's face it, Dr Laz is hardly likely to go trolling off to Brighton, not with his pussy in its current state.' He shifted in his seat, miming rectal discomfort, although in fact the actor playing the proctologist had stopped short of actual penetration, despite Terri's urgings.

'It's the oldest trick in the book. Big accident – bang! – wipes out half the cast, especially the less popular ones. Worked wonders for *Emmerdale*.'

'But Terri, what about my contract?' said Leah Wilkinson, briefly back in the show after a lengthy spell in rehab. 'They can't just sack me.'

'Oh, my dear,' said Terri, turning on his least favourite cast member, 'they can. Contracts have this nasty little habit of expiring. You really should get someone to read these things before you make your mark on them.'

'Well that's not what I heard,' said Tim Boreham, who got most of his 'inside' information from *New Town* fansites and messageboards.

'And what, pray, is the underclass saying about us?' said Terri, lighting a cigarette in flagrant breach of the rules.

'OK, the inside track is that there's going to be a fire at the launderette, Maggie gets caught in the office, flames all around her, Bernard goes in to rescue her, tells her he loves her, they have a big snog as the roof collapses on them, cliffhanger, pick-up in next episode probably straight after the news, firemen arrive, whole place explodes, setting fire to Dawn and Dave's flat, just as she's having an affair with Dean, or was it Vince?'

'Are you sure about that?' asked Tyrone, who had been practising hip-hop dance moves for a youth centre scene to be shot that afternoon.

'Yeah, I think so,' said Tim. 'Unless… hang on a minute, that might have been in the fan fiction section…'

'Christ, you are a tedious little person,' said Terri. 'Now, Tyrone, try extending the legs when you're lying on your back. That's it. And thrust the pelvis, five and six and seven and eight, then flip over on all fours.'

'Leave the poor kid alone, you dirty old queen,' said Leah, stalking off towards the loo.

'Why, oh, why won't she just overdose?'

'And the sooner they kill you off with bum cancer the better.'

'Listen, you large-breasted dwarf, nothing would make me happier than a valedictory deathbed scene followed by a comfortable dotage on my enormous Channel Six pension. Now fuck off and shoot up, and leave the professionals in peace.'

A large black BMW turned off Bromley Road and continued its sinister progress along the characterless suburban street that led to the *New Town* lot. It passed a small, ever-present gaggle of truant schoolgirls who peered at the smoked-glass windows, hoping for a glimpse of their screen favourites. They saw only the dim outline of a middle-aged woman and returned to their fizzy drinks and texting.

The car paused at the gatehouse, a name was muttered to the security guard, the barrier was raised. It purred, silent but deadly, behind the lot to the featureless six-storey bunker that housed the production offices. It stopped, and the driver opened the door for a chic, fiftysomething woman, all tailored elegance and D&G shades, who stepped purposefully across the threshold, her alligator briefcase tucked under her arm like an automatic weapon.

'I'd rather go in a blaze of glory than just slink off quietly in the back of a cab.'

'I think there's precious little chance of you doing anything in a blaze of glory, dear.' Terri was undermining another victim, this time Tricia Marvell, who played – but for how much longer? – Maggie's errant daughter Hayley.

'But Hayley has always been one of the most popular characters in the show. I do loads of supermarkets and stuff.'

'Always has been, dear, with the emphasis on the "has-been". But think about it. When did you last have a really good storyline?'

'Oh, for heaven's sake, she's carrying the child of the man who raped her.'

'Such vieux chapeau, don't you think? Not what the new producer likes at all…'

'New producer?'

'New producer, new broom. I'd start looking for that taxi if I were you, dear…'

*

'Here to see Nick Needs.'

'Who shall I say is…?'

'Sonia Sutherland.'

'Do you have an…?'

'Sonia!' Nick Needs rushed forward from the lift. 'Great to see you!' It was the first time he had ever met anyone in reception.

'Excuse me, madam, you need a pass.'

Sonia Sutherland glared at the receptionist. 'You're sacked,' she said.

'That's Sonia Sutherland. I've worked with her on *Path Lab*,' said one of the sparks to one of the grips. 'She's a fucking Rottweiler.'

'Face like one too. Nice tits, though,' said the grip, supping on a styrofoam cup of tea.

'Forget it, mate,' said the sparks. 'Not a chance.'

'What's she doing here, then?'

'New boss, I reckon. Christ, they must really be in trouble.'

Marjorie Mayhew breezed past on her way into make-up. The publicist, who was trying to persuade her to talk to *Saga* magazine, tottered in her wake.

'And I'm delighted to hear that the new producer is a very old friend of mine. We worked together on so many marvellous things in the '70s when television was really television. He's a lovely man, so I'm safe as houses. Such a nice feeling, when all around you are in such a precarious position. Oh, tell the old biddies to sod off; it's not as if I need the publicity.'

'Fuck,' said Sonia Sutherland, casting a basilisk glare down from the producer's office, where she was unzipping her case. 'Is that old hen Marjorie Mayhew still in the show? Better bump her off good and quick.'

'Well, like I said, Sonia, you've got a blank sheet of paper in front of you,' said Nick Needs. 'What you write on it is entirely up to you.'

'Too right,' said Sonia Sutherland, pacing her new office with an already-proprietorial air. 'Sonia Sutherland does things her way.' She had acquired the habit of referring to herself in the third person from reading too many laudatory articles in the quality press, who loved her 'hard-hitting' dramatic style. This usually meant that, in any Sutherland production, several prostitutes got carved up and wrapped in polythene sheeting, some children got terrorised by gruesome nonces and lots of actors that you'd seen somewhere but you weren't sure where said things like ''E's fucking stiffed, guv'. For this kind of gory nonsense she had been handsomely rewarded by an industry in search of sensation; most recently she had steered Channel Six's lame hospital drama *Path Lab* to success by introducing long, loving close-ups of maggot-infested wounds.

If anyone could save *New Town*, said the grapevine, it was Sonia Sutherland. She repeated this to herself several times a day.

'Top of my head, Nick,' she said, feeling the familiar warm rush of creativity, 'I'd say serial killer. New towns are full of 'em. Got any foreigners in the cast? Play on the fear factor. Asylum-seekers carving up old grannies. Put that old mare out to grass with a knife in her windpipe.'

Nick Needs shuddered with fear. But he could see his revenue gap closing before his very eyes.

'…and of course you know that she's a good friend of your favourite person, Gavin Graham. Wouldn't be surprised if she brings him in.'

'Over my dead body,' said Eileen, who knew far more about the new regime at *New Town* than she was prepared to let on to Terri. 'That bastard has always had it in for me.'

'That's not what they're saying, dear. He was all over you at that gorgeous party we had for pretty boy's birthday.'

'I told him where to get off.'

'Not what I heard, Eileen.'

'If I were you, Terri my old love, I'd keep my ruby-red nose out of other people's business.'

'Gavin said that Jimmy was holding you back.'

'Terri,' said Eileen, 'if I hear that you've been talking out of turn, I'll shove that proctoscope so far up your wrinkled old arsehole that you'll be singing descant in the Christmas choir, do you understand me?'

'All too well, mistress,' hissed Terri, who knew that Eileen seldom threatened without the muscle to back it up. 'Just trying to be a pal.'

'Understood.'

'Well,' said Terri five minutes later to the first person he could get to listen, 'when I mentioned Gavin Graham's name, she jumped down my throat, dear, I tell you. There's more to this than meets the eye.'

And there was.

Shooting was suspended for an hour the following afternoon – something that normally happened only for the death of a monarch – and the entire staff were summoned to Studio One, where a small stage and lectern had been erected. By this time actorish speculation had reached critical mass, and there were reports of signs and wonders around the *New Town* lot, as in the last days of Rome. T. J. Daniels swore he'd seen a spectral line through his head in the latest rushes, but that was probably an acid flashback.

News of Sonia Sutherland's arrival had swept the green room, and those who knew of her reputation (there were few who didn't) had a pretty good idea of what to expect. In general, the buzz was good. Sonia Sutherland had a reputation as a starmaker, and she'd already helped Damian Davies to make the transition from *New Town* poster boy to real-life actor thanks to a leading role in *Path Lab*. Like all actors, the *New Town* cast longed to run down rain-soaked, blue-lit London streets wielding firearms and saying 'fuck' a lot. All of this, Sonia Sutherland could deliver.

Nick Needs quelled the babble with a papal hand gesture and spoke to the assembled cast for the first time in years; some of them had never actually heard his voice before.

'Friends, colleagues…' he began.

'Who's she trying to kid?' hissed Terri into Marjorie's ear. Since hearing of the new appointment, neither was as confident as before.

'You'll doubtless have heard that Tracey has chosen to step down from the hot seat.'

'She "stepped down" in the same way Tosca did,' whispered Terri, who was silenced by the beady eye of Sutherland.

'And I'm sure you'll join me in wishing her the very best with an exciting new raft of projects that she's developing for the independent sector.' Nick burbled on for a minute or two before getting to the point. 'And so it gives me great pleasure to welcome to *New Town* a woman who is quite literally a legend in her own lifetime. Ladies and gentlemen, I give you Sonia Sutherland.'

It was starting to sound like the build-up to a nightclub act, so the actors gave Sonia a hearty round of applause.

Sonia drew herself up to the lectern like a cobra preparing to strike.

'Right,' she said, scanning the ranks, 'Sonia Sutherland is here, and things are going to change.' Her voice was cracked and smoky. 'I don't know what you've heard or what you've been saying...' She raked the audience with her heavy-lidded brown eyes and came to rest on Terri. 'But all of it is true.'

There was a gasp from the assembled cast, who recognised a great actress when they saw one. Mentally they started going over their pension arrangements.

'And just so there's no doubt, I'll spell out exactly what's going to happen in Sonia Sutherland's *New Town*. Brace yourselves.'

An assistant director ran around the room with handouts while Sonia paced the stage, her hands behind her back. She was dressed in a smartly tailored, camel-coloured jacket and trousers, with just a hint of scarf to soften the otherwise dykey ensemble.

'Quiet.'

They obeyed.

'Now listen, and listen good. There's a killer on the loose, and it ain't Sonia Sutherland.' This was starting to sound like dialogue from one of her over-budgeted thrillers, but the audience was lapping it up, stealing sidelong glances as if the 'killer' might strike at any moment.

'Turn to page one.' There was a rustle of paper and another gasp as the actors saw the word MURDER in twenty-four-point bold.

'Yeah,' leered Sonia, 'murder. The original crime, the only crime that matters. The only drama that anybody really wants to watch.' She had done this routine at so many pitching meetings that she now believed it herself.

'And who's gonna die first?' Again she scanned the room, searching for a victim. The tension was unbearable; Tyrone actually wet his pants.

'Ladies and gentlemen,' she continued, as if announcing an award, 'our first corpse is…Vince!'

Every head in the room snapped round to focus on T. J. Daniels, who was snoozing in the back row, as was his habit when the cameras weren't rolling.' Someone wake him up and tell him he's dead,' said Sonia, relishing this macabre turn of events.

'But who would do a thing like that?' asked Gemma, already caught up in the drama. 'Vince ain't hurt no one.'

'That's where you're wrong, babe,' said Sonia. 'Listen and learn.'

And so she outlined a new direction for *New Town*, a direction that would close the gap between budget and revenue, and which would send the ratings rocketing – but at what cost?

'First of all, Vince is a beast.' Sonia used words like 'beast' without irony. 'What do we really know about his past? Where did he come from? What was he doing before he arrived in Eastgate as a window-cleaner? I'll tell you.' She paused for dramatic effect. 'He was in prison.'

Even T. J. was awake now.

'And why, you ask? Because he'd killed his missus.'

There was a deathly hush.

'Vince is a nasty piece of work. He's a wife-beater. An alcoholic. A drug dealer. He's done time. He knows some villains. He tried to start a new life in Eastgate, but the past has a way of catching up with us, doesn't it? And before long he's under pressure from his old cronies to pull a new job, and he takes the stress out on Maggie by knocking her about a bit.'

'Ooh!'

'And there comes a point when she just can't take it any more. She snaps.'

'She kills him!' squeaked Gemma.

'Or does she? You see, there's someone else who wants Vince dead. A couple of people, in fact. First up, there's Dean. He can't stand to see his mother bruised and bleeding in every episode, and we know he's a violent little bastard – gets that from his dad.' Her eyes settled on Benjamin Oluwatobi, who had actually forgotten that his character, Bernard Johnson, was Dean's father, after a short-lived mixed-race liaison with Maggie, a storyline that was curtailed after Channel Six was bombarded with hate mail from extreme right-wing organisations.

'But Bernard's not a violent man,' said Benjamin, somewhat affronted. 'He would never kill anyone.'

'Not so far,' said Sonia, who couldn't bear to see a black character without a good old-fashioned black storyline. 'But that was before he got involved in child trafficking.'

Those members of the cast who understood what child trafficking meant looked deeply uneasy.

'Bernard's got this cousin, see, who comes over from Nigeria or wherever they're from, and he's into some heavy voodoo shit and needs children for human sacrifice. He puts a curse on Bernard and forces him to start procuring kiddies for him, because if he doesn't he's going to take Bernard's own children on a "holiday" to Nigeria from which they will never return.'

Sonia was savouring every word, and the audience was on the edge of its seat.

'So Bernard turns to the one man in Eastgate he knows is dodgy enough to get hold of kids for money.'

'But this is ridiculous,' said Benjamin. 'How would a law-abiding man like Bernard know anything about Vince's underworld connections?'

'He's got contacts in the 'hood, hasn't he? Think about it. A black man living in a town like that, he's going to know where to go if he wants a job done. Stands to reason.'

Benjamin walked out of the room.

'And then there were two,' hissed Sonia. 'So who was it? Who killed Vince Palmer? Was it Eileen, killed him in anger because she couldn't take any more beatings? Or was it Dean, sick of seeing his mother smashed in the face, and possibly sick of being fiddled with by his uncle Vince as well?' This idea has only just occurred to her, but it seemed too good to waste. 'Or was it Bernard, the man of peace driven to a desperate act when Vince failed to procure kiddies for his gruesome voodoo ritual?'

'Tell us! Tell us!' cried Gemma.

'Not on your nelly, mate,' said Sonia. 'You lot will be the last to know. I know what actors are like. Can't keep their mouths shut.'

'But my dear, we do read the scripts,' said Terri.

'Yeah,' said Sonia, 'and that's why we're filming three different endings.'

'Oooooh!'

'And…'

'Yes?'

'We're filming them abroad.'

The revolution was complete. Sonia Sutherland was in control.

When the dust had settled and the cast had gone back to work, Sonia took a blank sheet of paper and started writing. This is what she wrote. She was a very organised woman.

actor	character	pro	con	action
Eileen Weathers	Maggie Parrott	Top publicity. Can act. +++ violence	May go to prison soon	Keep. Offer more £££
Terence Lee	Dr Lazarus Ditchling	Popular. Can act. Near retirement	Irritating old poof with vicious tongue	Keep if he keeps his mouth shut
Marjorie Mayhew	Poppy Ditchling	Older viewers? No, fuck 'em	Tired, ugly, boring, posh	Kill off character, sack MM
Tim Boreham	David Ditchling	May take pay cut to stay in	Boring wanker	??? serial killer storyline???
Tricia Marvell	Hayley Ditchling	Nice tits	Can't act	Murder (DD's first victim?). Sack. CHECK CONTRACT
Benjamin Oluwatobi	Bernard Johnson	Black; useful to have in show	Boring nigger	Keep: +++ voodoo storyline

Tyrone D	Dean Parrott	Cute. Teen/ gay interest. Can dance	Can't act	??? Strictly Come Dancing?
Leah Wilkinson	Amanda Parrott	Thick & cute	Mouthy	FHM shoot
Steve Seddon	Dave Stannard-Watson	Hunk. Good for gay audience?	Has done porn. Can't act	Sack (poss use in Path Lab?)

At the bottom of the list, she scrawled the names T. J. Daniels and Gemma Leeds, bracketed them together and wrote 'Job Done'.

She left the page underneath a pile of folders on her desk. When she came in the next morning, it was still there. Little did Sonia know that it had been found, photocopied and returned. She wasn't quite organised enough.

Eileen and Terri shared a car into town at the end of the day's shooting.

'Business or pleasure, dear?' said Terri, rubbing moisturiser into his chubby hands as the car crawled along the A21.

'Little bit of both if all goes according to plan. Mum's the word for now, Terri, as I mentioned.'

'Oh, I see,' said Terri, rightly guessing that Eileen was on her way to a clandestine meeting with Gavin Graham. 'Well, I can't say I blame you. I'd be looking for a way out myself if I wasn't quite as ancient as I am.'

'And if you want to live to enjoy your retirement…'

'Silent as the grave, dear, don't you fret. Mind you, I thought we'd all had it this afternoon. What do you make of La Sutherland?'

Unlike the younger cast members, neither Eileen nor Terri was especially impressed by Sonia Sutherland. They'd seen producers come and go, although none as spectacularly bloodthirsty.

'Well, I'm just relieved that I'm not the victim, darlin', said Eileen. 'Although I must say I wouldn't mind being a killer.'

'Maggie a murderess? It doesn't seem likely, does it? What's she going to do? Drown him in fabric conditioner?'

'Think about it, though,' said Eileen. 'A big, violent scene for starters, lots of blood and guts. Then all the guilt, that's always fun to do. Then the arrest, the trial, big number in the witness box, and off to prison. I mean, it's every actress's dream! There'll be a "Free Maggie Parrott" campaign! Students will wear T-shirts with my face on them! Questions will be asked in Parliament, darlin'! Gives me a nice high profile just when I need it most.'

'Just when you're looking for a new job?'

'Just when I'm about to publish my book, darlin'.'

'But of course. Silly me.'

'Yes, a tasty little murder. That's how we used to sort things out down south London. Someone crossed your path…' She mimed slitting her throat. 'No questions asked.'

'Eileen, my dear,' said Terri, gathering his blouse around his wattles, 'you frighten me sometimes, you really do.'

chapter seven

Terri Lee wasn't the only one who was worried about Eileen. Even Paul, placated as he was by the irregular charverings he was getting off Danny, began to wonder if all was well with the nation's favourite laundress. She had become uncharacteristically efficient, and even gave the impression of having prepared for their ongoing interviews. This was good from the biographer's point of view, but it alarmed the novelist. Eileen had turned from a lovable cockney scatterbrain into something resembling a proper soap villainess. There were phone calls which she walked out of the room to conduct. There were meetings at night, frequent text messages, couriers at the door. During one of Eileen's longer absences, Paul whipped out his notebook and jotted down a thousand words of notes for a novel in which extracts from a bland showbiz biography were interspersed with snippets of taped conversations that undermined the façade of accepted truth… and then he saw Danny doing something technical to the pool's filtration system, and his mind seemed to wander.

Despite Eileen's apparent change of personality, the book was progressing well. They had covered Eileen's childhood, the disappearance of her father, the formative years at her Nana Scammell's on Walworth Road, and had concocted a colourful chapter on Eileen's teenage shenanigans as an emergent south London sexpot. It was cheerfully, bawdily frank, and it revealed a self-deprecating sense of humour that, thought Paul, should go over well with the critics. They covered the later 1960s in some depth: how

Eileen left Nana Scammell's home in 1966 and got a flat in Charlotte Street with two other girls, an actress and a stripper, how she'd scraped a living as an artist's model, picking up her clients (all of whom were now incredibly famous, collectable and dead) in the pubs of Fitzrovia. She painted a seductive picture of stockings drying over the backs of bentwood chairs, of shared suppers cooked over a single gas-ring on the landing, of camaraderie and high jinks that stopped just short of wickedness. Paul had to do very little other than take out the ums and ahs, put the anecdotes into some kind of rational order and correct the more obvious howlers. Although he had absolutely no feedback from Six Books, he was confident that, between them, he and Eileen were doing a grand job.

Yet every so often the niggling maggot of doubt gnawed at the apple of autobiography. How much could he really believe? Was she stringing him along for her own purposes? And did it really matter? A few weeks ago, he would have been content to take the money and run – off to Paris, or somewhere equally suitable, to write whichever of his many novels seemed most promising at the time, preferably with Danny in tow. But now he had started to care – about the truth, about literature, about the reading public. Was he peddling a pack of lies? Should he confront Eileen with his doubts? But he never did. He had fallen under Eileen's spell, like Edmund in *The Lion, the Witch and the Wardrobe*. Instead of Turkish delight, she had snared him with Danny, who was half-Maltese but entirely delightful.

So Paul kept his worries to himself and did as he was told. The project was running to schedule, the money was rolling in and Eileen seemed happy and fulfilled. This was surprising, considering that her marriage was on the rocks, but there was no ignoring the fact that the woman was blooming. Her frankness in interviews extended to the subject of her husband, about whom she spoke without rancour.

'I might as well tell you, darlin', by the time this book of ours comes out I won't be Mrs Jimmy Livesey any more. Poor Jimmy, he's like a dog, he can't help sniffing round lampposts. I don't blame him; he's a man, and men are led by their dicks. I've led a few of them myself, so I can't really complain.'

Even when the *Daily Herald* ran a story in which Gemma Leeds spoke openly about her "real-life" romance with sizzling screen stud Jimmy Livesey (and modelled some nasty catalogue lingerie in the accompanying photographs), Eileen remained sanguine. 'She's a silly tart, but I can't hate her,' she told Paul the morning after the story appeared. 'She's a lot like me. Grew up on the streets, but she never really left them…That's the difference between us.'

In Paul's eyes, this stoical acceptance of suffering sealed Eileen's iconic status. When she spoke of herself as a woman past the age for love, grateful for a full and happy life and looking to a calm if lonely future, he almost had to brush away a tear. She was so brave, so wise, and in her own way, so moral…

And then there was the fire.

Paul spent a long time piecing together events leading up to this 'TV tragedy', as the papers called it, not least because he was required to do so by the police. He had been chez Eileen in the morning as usual, taping two hours of interviews before she was collected by the car that took her to the *New Town* lot. It was a couple of weeks after the Gemma Leeds story broke, and Jimmy had more or less moved out of the Essex mansion in order to live with his mistress in Primrose Hill. He still kept his belongings in the marital home, however, and would return from time to time to collect things he needed (to sell, according to Eileen). This he did when his wife was out; it was an arrangement less painful to both.

Eileen had seemed, that morning, to be in good spirits, neither elated nor depressed, although complaining of a headache which she blamed on lack of sleep. No, she had not been excitable or distracted. No, there had been no mysterious phone calls. The tapes themselves, when played back and scrutinised, yielded no hint of anything amiss. She had spoken with great fondness of her first break on the London stage, appearing in a tiny part in *There's a Girl in My Soup*. She had taken Paul on a verbal tour of 1960s Soho, the Maltese cafés, the gangsters and pimps and drag queens and artists who crowded the pavements in those dear, dead days. She spoke of Mediterranean holidays paid for by boyfriends who were far too gentlemanly to lay a hand on her ('although I wouldn't have minded much if they did, darlin'!') and of her first tentative steps into television as a bikini-clad showgirl. It was good, solid stuff, remarkable for nothing other than Eileen's skills as a raconteur. Even the investigating officer at Harlow police station had laughed and said he looked forward to receiving a signed copy of the book.

After Eileen had gone to work, Paul ate lunch in the kitchen with Danny, as was now their habit, and then, instead of returning to London, passed the afternoon in Danny's nearby flat. They shared a bottle of wine and spent an hour or so…well, Paul didn't like to say 'fucking' to a police officer. And afterwards? They had slept, of course. That, said Danny, was one of the great things about doing it with other blokes; they didn't want to talk about 'us' for the next two hours.

When Paul awoke, it was already dark, and Danny was emerging from the shower. 'Time to get up, Sleeping Beauty,' he'd said, ruffling Paul's hair. 'I'll take you to the station. Get a move on.'

Thanks to some speedy driving, Paul got the 18.34 up train and was back in his Waterloo home when he saw the news on the internet.

STAR'S COUNTRY HOUSE BLAZE ran the headline. 'Emergency services have been in attendance at the Essex home of soap star Eileen Weathers this afternoon. A fire was reported at the house just after 4pm, destroying most of one wing before it was brought under control an hour later. Police say that the house was occupied at the time but have not yet released details of any casualties.'

He immediately called Danny – his first thought being, irrationally, that he may have been hurt, although he knew perfectly well that he was with him at the time the fire broke out. There was no reply from the flat, and Danny's mobile was switched off, and so, in a panic, Paul rang the Essex mansion itself. Jimmy's voice answered.

'Hello,' it said, 'Eileen and Jimmy can't come to the phone right now. Please leave a message after the tone and we'll get back to you.'

He hung up, and the phone immediately rang. It was the police.

It took them a long time to get round to telling him the bad news. Yes, there had been people in the house at the time of the fire. No, there had been no survivors. No, they could not yet reveal which part of the house the fire had started in. Yes, firefighters had worked non-stop to break into the room where they believed two people had been trapped. And then, finally, when Paul was near hysteria, they told him that two bodies had been recovered from the smouldering rubble.

Jimmy Livesey and Gemma Leeds. Burned to a crisp.

Paul spent an hour mechanically pumping Danny's number into his phone. Finally, he got an answer.

'Hang on, lover. She's here. She wants to talk to you.'

'But Danny, are you OK?'

''Ello, darlin'. It's me.' Eileen's voice sounded cracked and tired, as if she had inhaled smoke.

'Where are you?'

'I'm at the house. What's left of it.'

'Oh, Eileen, I'm so sorry. I just heard the news.'

'It's awful. I don't know what I'm going to do without them.'

'How did they get trapped?'

'I don't know, Paul. They shouldn't have been there. I mean, they'd had their dinner and everything as usual.'

'It's a tragedy, Eileen. If there's anything…'

'They must have got back into the house somehow.'

'Well, he had a key, didn't he…?'

'And then when the fire got a grip they panicked and hid somewhere and suffocated in the smoke. I can't bear it.'

Eileen's voice teetered on the brink of tears.

'Oh, Eileen…' Paul couldn't think of anything to say.

'They hadn't hurt anybody.' She was now weeping openly, and Paul could hear Danny's voice in the background, asking for his phone back.

'It's not fuckin' fair,' wailed Eileen, breaking down. 'My poor little Chocolate and Biscuit. My poor little doggies…'

'Paolo,' said Danny's voice, 'I'm taking her to the hospital now. She's in shock. Don't call for a couple of days, mate. I'll be in touch.'

'I love you,' blurted Paul, overcome by the drama of it all, but the line had already gone dead.

The devastation at the Essex mansion was truly horrifying. The fire had spread fast, making quick work of the fixtures and fittings, catching on to the wood of the staircase until there was an inferno. Jimmy and Gemma never stood a chance. They had been down in Jimmy's 'rumpus room', as Eileen called it, where he had his sound system and his home cinema and the rest of his expensive hardware. It didn't take much to imagine what they'd been up to in there; when the bodies had been discovered, said firemen, they were entwined like the victims of Pompeii, desperately clinging one to another as they awaited a fate they could not escape.

While the fury of the fire seemed to have concentrated on its victims, the rest of the house had not escaped. The living room, where Paul and Eileen had spent so many happy hours in conversation, was a blackened shell. The furniture went up like a torch, alongside priceless *objets d'art* and filing cabinets full of Eileen's personal belongings. Fortunately, she'd had the sense to entrust her photograph albums to the picture researchers at Six Books; otherwise they too would have been lost. But the damage was bad enough: letters, scrapbooks, driving licence, even her passport and birth certificate, had been reduced to ashes.

And most poignant of all was the loss of Eileen's beloved spaniels, found asphyxiated in a kitchen cupboard where they had run for safety from the flames. It was this discovery that had finally snapped Eileen's fragile self-control, and she spent the next forty-eight hours under heavy sedation at a private hospital.

Paul was unable to speak either to her or to Danny and spent his days in a strange, depressing limbo. Emma from Six Books phoned at the end of the week, having 'just heard the awful news' and wondering 'if this means that you'll be late delivering the rest of the – what do you call it? – copy'. Paul retained his composure and said he thought that, by and large, there might be a slight delay. Emma seemed cross.

Eileen surfaced five days after the fire, during which time press coverage had reached a crescendo of pity and speculation. How had the fire started, they all wanted to know? Was it a 'kinky love game' that had gone wrong, asked the *Beacon*? They hinted of 'long sessions' involving 'hot candle wax' that could have sparked the cataclysm. The *Herald* maintained the high ground, asking 'who called 999?' and wondering why the emergency services had not been alerted until the fire had spread to every part of the house. But they all agreed, whatever their standard bias, that we should all feel jolly sorry for Eileen Weathers, who had already lost her husband to another woman but didn't need to see him going up in smoke. Jokes flew around the *New Town* lot that at least she'd been spared the expense of a divorce. 'Not to mention a cremation,' added Terri.

Sonia drew a line through Gemma's name on her list. Cheaper than sacking her, she thought.

A press statement was issued to the effect that Eileen would be returning to work as soon as the doctors said she was well enough, and that she was determined 'not to let her public down'.

Paul waited for a call that never came. He tried to speak to the *New Town* publicists, but they treated him as if he was some sleazy tabloid hack. Danny's mobile number had not been recognised for a week, then two weeks, then three. By the time a month had elapsed, Paul was resigned to his fate. He delivered what copy he could to Six Books and invoiced them for the second instalment of his money, claiming, rightly, that he had worked to the best of his ability. With the cheque in his pocket, he bought an open return on Eurostar and decamped to Paris with a stock of A4 pads and a large supply of pens.

He spent the first week in a Montmartre sauna, the second in his hotel room furiously engaged in online chat, and returned to London broke and exhausted. His pads were full of scribbled notes, outlines for possible novels, unposted letters to Danny and hundreds of unused telephone numbers.

chapter eight

The voice on the phone was unmistakable.

'You are coming with us to Malta, aren't you, darlin'?'

Paul had heard nothing from Eileen for two months after the fire and had been forced, like the rest of humanity, to follow her story through the press, picking out some version of the truth between the wildly differing stories in the *Beacon* and the *Herald*. The *Beacon* stuck doggedly to the official line: the fire was a ghastly accident, Eileen had lost everything, and it was all the fault of her feckless, drink and drug-addicted husband and his floozy mistress, who, by implication, deserved to die. The *Herald*, never a paper to miss an opportunity to knock *New Town* and its media owners, took the side of the deceased and paid a great deal of money to Gemma Leeds's 'tragic mum', 'tragic sister' and 'tragic baby brother'. 'Our Gemma was a lovely, bright, bubbly girl with her whole life ahead of her, and that's been taken away,' said the grieving (but much wealthier) mother. 'We demand justice for Gemma,' said the sister, a practical girl who hoped to parlay this family tragedy into a television career. They didn't come right out and say it, because the lawyers objected, but they hinted that Eileen Weathers was in some way to blame for Gemma's death. They let it be known that a large amount of compensation would soften the blow.

Paul also read that *New Town*'s new boss Sonia Sutherland was taking the principal cast to an 'undisclosed foreign location' for a story 'that would put *New Town* back on the map'. 'It's a classic soap drama,' Sutherland told anyone who would listen, 'with violence, murder, incest and gangsters.' The papers speculated as to whether or not Eileen Weathers was well enough to leave the country (the *Beacon*) or whether the police should allow her to leave (the *Herald*). Knowing Eileen, thought Paul, she'd got a replacement passport and would be on the first plane out.

'Am I?' stammered Paul. 'Well, I suppose I am, then.'

'Course you are, darlin'!' laughed Eileen, her voice fully restored to its resonant south London glory. 'Lots to tell!'

'So does this mean the book's back on, then?'

'Back on, darlin'? It was never off!'

'I just thought that…Well, when you didn't call…'

'Sorry about that, Paul. Had a lot on my mind. You know, throwing myself into my work, finding a place to live, organising the funeral and all that.'

Paul was still in a sulk about the funeral; he felt, as did his friends, that he should have been invited. These friends were starting to treat him with a little less respect than he had become used to.

'Well, I don't know if I can drop everything just like that. I mean, I'm in the middle of a new novel, and it's in a really interesting…'

'Danny's coming.'

'When do we leave?'

Eileen made it sound so easy, but it had been far from. Behind the scenes at *New Town*, she had been subjected to the kind of interrogation that went out with the Star Chamber.

'We support you, Eileen, we recognise your value to the show, you're our touchstone, the viewers love you…' rambled Nick Needs, all of which sounded like prefatory remarks to a sacking.

'The bottom line,' broke in Sonia Sutherland, a woman of few words, 'is did you kill Jimmy and Gemma or not?'

Level gaze met level gaze. Sonia and Eileen were well matched, and under different circumstances would have liked each other. At the moment, however, each saw the other as a threat.

'No, I didn't,' said Eileen. 'Did you?'

The staring match went on a little longer.

'The police say it was an accident,' said Eileen.

'That's not an answer.'

'The coroner's inquest returned a verdict of death by misadventure.'

'I'm waiting,' said Sonia.

'All right, then. If I must. I won't forget this, Sonia. No, I did not kill my husband. No, I did not get anyone else to kill my husband. No, I can't think of nobody who wanted my husband dead, because even though he was a stupid dickhead he didn't deserve to die. I lost my home, remember, and my dogs.'

'The papers have suggested...' began Nick.

'I know what the papers have suggested, darlin'. That I did it for the insurance money. Well, yes, that's a possible motive, I suppose, because everything was well insured, as you advised me several times. But why would I need the money? Because I had secret debts? Because – oh yes, I remember this now – because I was being blackmailed by someone who knew me back in the days when I was a boy and threatened to bring new evidence to light?'

'Wow, is that true?' said Nick.

'If you ever ask me a question like that again, not only will I walk off the show, but I will land you in such deep shit that you will wish you'd been born without a mouth.'

'I don't know what you mean.'

'Shut up, Nick,' said Sonia. 'She's right.' Sonia knew what Nick didn't – that Eileen was now working closely with super-PR-man Gavin Graham, and that any attempt to cross her would result in a welter of negative publicity for the show. This was not a time when *New Town* could ride out such storms; it was clinging to a prime-time slot by its fingernails.

'However, if it helps you to feel better, I will sign a bit of paper saying I didn't kill my husband. I will give an exclusive to the broadsheet newspaper of your choice about how the press coverage of the tragedy nearly destroyed me. I will do whatever you want me to – but only if I feel I've got your absolute one hundred per cent trust and confidence, darlin'.'

'Well…'

Sonia knew better than to bargain. 'It's a deal.'

The two women shook hands, and the question of Eileen's culpability in the death of her husband was never mentioned again. With Channel Six fully behind her, and with Gavin Graham issuing statements and counter-statements behind the scenes, the rumours were soon extinguished, leaving only a few public-house jokes and a vague, sexy whiff of scandal as Jimmy's final legacy.

With that little misunderstanding cleared up, Sonia went on to describe the sensational new storyline she had up her sleeve for Maggie and co. They would go on a family holiday to Malta (cheap labour, guaranteed sun, ideal for filming), where, after much tension and glowering, Vince would be murdered.

It was audacious, it was sensational, it was entirely unsuitable for *New Town*'s family viewing slot, and thus, in Sonia's eyes, it was the perfect direction for the show to take.

Vince would plunge to his death from an extremely high cliff on Malta's tiny sister island of Gozo, where he had taken Maggie on a romantic, can't-we-try-again day trip. Did he fall or was he pushed? Silly question: the only mystery was, who had done it? Was it Maggie herself, sick of the lies and the beatings, who, after harsh words and a tussle on the cliff edge, sent him to a messy death on the rocks below? Was it Dean, who followed them over on the ferry, lay in wait until Vince was alone and attacked him in revenge for his mother's sufferings? Or was it – gasp! – Bernard Johnson, who, unknown to everyone, had stalked the family to Malta and cold-bloodedly murdered Vince for failing to deliver the children he required for his grim trade in voodoo sacrifice?

Sonia spelled all this out as if she was describing a normal trip to the launderette. Eileen and Nick, hardened soap professionals both, were on the edge of their seats.

'So?' they chorused as one. 'Who did it?'

Sonia rubbed her hands and chuckled. 'That's the beauty of it all,' she said. 'I don't know.'

'You…but…'

'We film three different endings. We give the story to the press. We milk it and milk it until the whole country is in a frenzy over Who Killed Vince? And then, when the time is right, when the ratings are through the roof, we make our minds up.'

'My God,' said Nick.

'Is it me?'

'Too early to tell, Eileen,' said Sonia. 'It all depends on Joe Public.'

'But how? Why?'

'It depends whether or not they believe that you could kill.'

In the two days between Eileen's call and their departure for Malta, Paul was showered with gifts and attention in a way that quite went to his head. Eileen sent him champagne in a beautiful leather travel-bag, couriered to his house from the *New Town* offices. Danny went one better and turned up at Paul's front door with the welcome announcement: 'I've got me toothbrush.'

When they all met at the airport, Eileen was in ebullient mood. 'I've never felt so positive about anything,' she announced, hugging Paul like a long-lost son. 'It's as if Jimmy's death has set me free. This book of ours is going to be something really special.' As they sipped cocktails in the first-class lounge, Eileen spoke of her ambitions to 'set the record straight' and to show the world that there was 'more to me than just a pretty face'.

'I see now that this book is the one thing I've been working towards all my life,' she told Paul, who, only days before, assumed that the project was dead in the water. 'You know, people can criticise my acting if they like, they can say I'm an old hag or a drunk or a slut. I wouldn't deny it, darlin'…' She nudged Paul in the ribs, and he spilled a little gin and tonic on his leg. Danny brushed it off. 'But one thing they can't take away from me is that I've had a fucking fabulous life. And thanks to you, Paul, I can finally show that to the world.' She brushed away a tear. 'Thank you for that, my darlin.''

The flight passed in a comfortable blur; Paul slept for much of the time with Danny's arm around his shoulders. He woke up at one point to hear the whispered words 'Gavin' and 'those bastards at Six', but then he was off again.

He only came to full consciousness as the plane touched down at Malta International Airport. Setting foot on the tarmac was one small step for Paul, but one giant leap away from his old life. He shouldn't have been there at all; he should, at that very moment, have been teaching a class on Edmund White. He had burned his bridges, broken faith with the college, told them he wouldn't be taking that week's class, nor the next, nor ever again in the foreseeable future, and if they had a problem with that they should have given him a contract on one of the many occasions he had begged for one. Now he was glad they hadn't. He was free, gloriously, giddily free.

The heat rose from the runway and smacked him in the face; Paul fumbled for his panama hat and shades. As a freckly, pale-skinned, weak-eyed Englishman, Paul found hot climates a challenge. Danny, on the other hand, being half-Maltese, was very much at home. He stretched, he smiled, he peeled off his T-shirt and began tanning instantly. By the time they reached the air-conditioned arrivals lounge, he was already several shades darker.

Eileen was doing the full showbiz number to the welcoming airport officials.

'Oh, Malta, Malta, my lovely Malta!' she husked. 'Yes, darlin', I'm back at last. Oh, thank you, how sweet,' she said to a wizened little lady who told her how satellite repeats of *New Town* kept her in touch with 'the old country'. She kissed an immigration official, gave autographs to children and passed through the airport like the visiting international superstar she apparently was. When she emerged into the blinding light of day, a smart black car was waiting to whisk her to her hotel. The limo door was opened from within; squinting through his shades into the expensive darkness, Paul recognised the handsome features of Gavin Graham.

'This is us, mate,' said Danny, leading Paul around the corner to the car park, where a large, powerful Japanese motorbike gleamed in the sun. 'Grab a helmet and hop on.'

Paul needed no second bidding, and within moments they were speeding down the dusty road towards the sea.

Paul and Danny were established, at Eileen's insistence and Channel Six's expense, at what can only be described as a gay love nest on the harbourfront at Sliema, a picturesque town with a long history of loucheness. From there they were free to explore the island on Danny's bike, which he rode mostly topless, Paul's arms around his waist. They could visit the location, or they could take long, leisurely lunches in any number of charming waterside restaurants, where Danny's impressive command of Maltese meant they were welcomed as honoured guests. It was far and away the happiest time of Paul's life.

The only constraints on their time were dictated by Eileen's filming schedule, because whenever she was not required on set she was busy dictating her memoirs. In the hazy heat of the unit base, where they sipped cold beer under the shade of an umbrella, or in the marble gloom of her hotel lobby, they talked, talked, talked. She spun yarns that would have lawyers' hair standing on end, dishing the dirt on every household name in light entertainment, a profession apparently stuffed with drug addicts, underage sex fiends, cross-dressers and high-profile necrophiliacs. Eileen recounted it all with relish.

'And when he dumped on her tits, she just leaned over and puked all over his cock! Well, that night they were on the Royal Variety Show, so they had a quick shower…

'…actually raised thousands of pounds for the hospital charity, but it was all a cover so that he could slip into the morgue at night…

'…didn't realise that the intercom had been left on, so the entire studio heard her screaming "Fuck me till I fart" at the top of her voice…

'…terrible old dyke, and didn't care who knew it…'

Not all of this would make the final cut, Paul knew – but when he got home, lightly tanned and well shagged, he would have enough to keep his new circle of friends in slavish rapture for months to come.

They moved through the early years of Eileen's career, her graduation from TV showgirl (via the obligatory stint as a Hill's Angel) to a high-profile role in a sitcom and her first taste of stardom.

They plumbed the depths of her difficult family situation, the permanent estrangement from her wayward mother, the close but tense relationship with a disapproving Nana Scammell, her worries for her younger sister Rose, already a mother in her teens. Transcribing the tapes on his balcony each morning, before the heat rose and with it Danny, Paul reflected on how very different his own young life had been. In the year of his birth, Eileen was running around town with gangster boyfriends, various of whom had killed, or been killed. By the time Paul started school, after an uneventful and secure childhood, Eileen was a household name. The biggest excitement of Paul's youth, apart from some unsatisfactory fumblings with nervous schoolmates, was a gap year during which he had interrailed around Europe and fallen in love with an Italian boy who romantically failed to turn up for their final date. After that, it fell depressingly into place: university, graduation, PhD, teaching, writing, first proper boyfriend, coming out to parents, first proper divorce, and then a tedious round of disappointments, both personal and professional. That was until Eileen Weathers blew into his life and turned it all upside down, inside out.

Now, at last, he was putting his talents to good use. Eileen told him every day what a 'great listener' he was. And Danny told him every night that he was 'a fantastic fuck', something Paul had long suspected but never had the chance to prove. He felt so happy that he forgot all those niggling doubts about the truth, literature and morality, and concentrated, for once, on living in the moment.

Eileen too was happier than Paul had ever seen her. She openly referred to herself as 'the Merry Widow' and was frank about her relief at being no longer married to Jimmy. They discussed this in a cocktail-fuelled heart to heart by Eileen's hotel pool, when she broke down in tears and admitted how guilty she felt – not, as Paul for a moment thought, about hiring a hit man, but about the immense sense of liberation she felt after Jimmy's death. Try as she might, she couldn't grieve. 'Perhaps it'll hit me one day, darlin',' she sobbed, 'but for now I'm having the time of my life.'

Malta suited Eileen, just as it suited Danny and, to his amazement, Paul. The air was clean, the sea, in which they bathed daily, was refreshing, the natives were as warm as the autumn sunshine. Eileen still knew people from her gangster heyday – family and friends of those fabulous, legendary Soho crooks who had courted her and treated her to sunshine holidays back in the good old days. Danny too knew people, constantly running into men around the harbour whom he would greet with a complicated handshake. Paul was occasionally jealous; some of those Maltese lads were almost as sexy as Danny, but he had little cause to worry. At worst, Danny was scoring the odd bit of dope, which seemed only to add to his sexual stamina, and going off for long, helmetless bike rides in the cool of the evening.

All in all they were a happy little family, and the word from the rushes was that Eileen was performing better than ever before. There was talk of Best Actress nominations at the Baftas. There were mutterings of a starring role in a British gangster flick, for which this was just an audition. Everywhere she went, she was greeted by adoring fans; Maltese telly, Paul figured, can't have been very good, because everyone on the island appeared to watch satellite reruns of *New Town*. Even the cabbies greeted her as 'Mag-geee!' Paul felt famous by association.

And there was another reason for Eileen's sudden happiness and energy, as she confided to Paul late one night. She was getting 'the shag of a lifetime' off Gavin Graham, her new publicist and constant companion.

Paradise lasted a week before the serpent appeared.

Thanks to Malta's laid-back attitude to the world in general, and current affairs in particular, there was no great appetite for news. The English newspapers arrived a day late, but only at shops where tourists were likely to go. And so it was some time before the whispering began. Danny nearly got into a fist fight when he overheard a red-faced Englishman saying to his hairy wife that 'I reckon they'll arrest that Eileen Weathers any day now, and just as well', adding that she had 'fled' the scene of the crime and that it was 'the girl's family that I feel sorry for'. Unaware of Danny's close involvement with Eileen, he developed his theme in the most unflattering language, most of it gleaned from a *Herald* leader.

'That's a friend of mine you're talking about, mate,' interrupted Danny.

'What?'

'Eileen Weathers. A friend of mine.'

Red Face looked Danny up and down – the tattoos over tanned muscles, the broken nose, the skinhead crop – but forged on regardless.

'You should be more careful how you pick your friends, then. Mate.'

'Meaning what?' said Danny, curling his fists. Paul could smell the testosterone on the hot, fennel-scented air.

'Meaning that you don't want to be hanging around with a murderer who's on the run from justice.'

'Say that again and see where it gets you.'

'You wouldn't dare.'

'Try me.'

Mrs Red Face was restraining her husband; Paul was restraining his. He thought he might scream with sheer excitement. The manager of the bar stepped out on to the patio.

'Is everything all right, gentlemen?'

'Yeah,' said Danny. 'I just don't like the smell of shit. C'mon, Paul.'

'Poofs,' muttered Mrs Red Face, mopping her husband's dripping brow.

They sped off on the motorbike, with the words 'police', 'poofs' and 'Maltese scum' lost on the wind behind them.

Eileen wasn't having much fun either. Since her arrival, she had been aware of cameras watching her every move; this she put down to the entirely natural interest of the Maltese media in a visiting superstar. But as the lenses got longer, she began to realise that these were not just domestic snappers. Photographers lined the road from hotel to location; they camped out on hilltops above the location; they haunted the hotel bar; they even posed as chambermaids and waiters. Eileen began to feel persecuted.

'What's going on?' she asked Gavin Graham, who smiled and patted her on the behind (two days later the picture ran as 'proof' of Eileen's 'new romance', with 150 words of disapproving copy). 'Don't you worry about a thing, babe. It's all under control.'

'But Gavin, darlin', these fucking cameras are everywhere. It's getting stupid.'

'Like I say, babe, all under control.'

Back in London, Sonia Sutherland scoured each day's papers for stories about

New Town in general, about Malta in particular and about Eileen's 'outrageous' disrespect for the Leeds family most eagerly of all. As the indignation mounted, and the 'calls' for Eileen to 'face justice' got louder, Sonia began to think that the public would accept Eileen as a killer very well indeed. It didn't matter that the police and the coroner were satisfied, that there was no official suspicion of foul play. The press smelled blood and came in for the kill.

Sonia sent a text to Gavin Graham.

'Well done.'

Principal shooting for the murder took place outside the small resort town of Xlendi, once a fishing village on the south-west corner of Gozo, now a cluster of cafés and restaurants around the pretty square bay where, in season, scuba divers and speedboat drivers stopped off for refreshment. Today, out of season, it was quiet, except for a bustle of activity in the car park, suddenly invaded by trailers and buses and lorries and the usual dreary bustle of location filming. Whatever the film, wherever the location, the creative and organisational hub is always a car park full of buses and lorries. There is always a smell of frying bacon.

Paul and Danny arrived on the ferry at ten, which was early for them; Danny was surly, having missed his morning swim, and Paul was in scarcely a better mood, having missed his morning shag. Eileen had been in make-up since seven and was as bright as a button. Gavin Graham hovered outside the trailer, making and receiving calls, occasionally wandering over to the 'production office' (another trailer) to check e-mails and faxes. The unit publicist, a Channel Six employee only because she was someone's daughter, tried to stop Paul and Danny at the barrier, asking for laminates and credentials. Danny pushed past her without a word, leaving Paul to bear the brunt of her wounded publicist's pride.

'You can't just come in off the streets and start nosing around, you know. This is a private film location.'

'I know. I'm a friend of Eileen's.'

'That's what they all say,' she said, brandishing her walkie-talkie. 'I'm calling security.'

'But you don't understand, I'm…'

'Hi, yah, problem at the gate. Some tourist trying to get in…'

Gavin Graham walked towards the barrier and stuck out a tanned, hairy hand. Had Paul not been so entirely Danny's slave, he would have liked to have been Gavin's.

'Paul Mackrell, right?'

'Yes.'

'Nice of you to come down, mate. I know Eileen's looking forward to seeing you.'

The unit publicist took her embarrassment out on the local security man, who went off and kicked a dog, so everyone had done their job.

'Well, darlin', today's the day,' said Eileen as Paul stumbled his way into the gloom of the make-up trailer, where Lorraine was working her cosmetic magic. 'What have you done with lover boy?'

'He's getting some breakfast.'

'God, he eats like a horse, that one. Don't know how he stays so thin. Must be all the calories he's burning off with you.'

Paul blushed prettily.

'Tell him I need him to run some errands for me, darlin',' said Eileen, as Lorraine put the finishing touches to Maggie's holiday tan and holiday black eye. 'I didn't just bring him out here to keep you satisfied, you know. He's meant to be working for a living.'

'Will do. Have we got time for a chat now?'

'Not now, Paul. I have to focus on the scene. It's my turn to murder T. J. today, darlin', and I don't want to fluff it.'

'So they really are filming three different endings, then?'

'Yeah, and they're all going to feature as extras on the DVD, innit?' said Lorraine. 'I bet it's Dean personally. I reckon he's a little hothead.'

'You reckon Tyrone's a little hothead, you mean, darlin',' said Eileen. 'Just remember you're old enough to be his mother.'

'I could teach him a trick or two. Come to mummy, baby…'

Paul left them to it and found Danny rounding off his breakfast with a coffee and a joint.

'She wants you, Danny.'

'Tell her she can wait.'

'Tell her yourself.' It was their first row, and Paul felt simultaneously tearful and elated. It meant they were a proper couple.

He was so distracted that he missed seeing Danny slipping in and out of the make-up trailer.

'I'm off for a ride, Paolo,' said Danny on his return; 'clear my head.'

'Aren't you going to watch the filming?'

'No, mate. Bores my tits off. I'll see you this afternoon for a spot of siesta, right?'

And he was off up the valley on the bike, a trail of dust settling on the thick beds of sugar cane that lined the road. Wild, impetuous boy, thought Paul, as he boarded the minibus heading out for the location. Eileen would follow in her own private car in order to maintain her focus.

The first port of call was an old watchtower that loomed out of the sandstone cliffs, shaped to soft curves by the sea breeze. It was a bit more than a breeze now; the stormy season was coming, and filming had occasionally been interrupted to allow the wind to die down. The scene was simple: Vince and Maggie, walking hand in hand along the cliffs where a few fellow trippers soaked up the sun, would discuss the ups and downs of their relationship and decide that, after all, they loved each other and would give it another go.

Paul watched from behind the cameras as Eileen and T. J. did take after take after take, cutting each time because of aeroplane noise, or wind noise, or the intrusion of some pesky local who had slipped through the cordon of assistant directors, runners and other flunkies. On the rare occasions when none of these things happened, T. J. fluffed his lines and persistently called Maggie 'Mary', even though he'd been acting with her for years. This, everyone knew, was the price you paid for a lifetime of substance abuse, but it did not make for easy filming. Eileen herself was consistent perfection on each and every take.

It took two hours to get that little scene in the can, then they moved on to another part of the island, where they would film the lovers' tiff that preceded

Vince's demise. By this time a growing crowd of locals and holidaymakers had sniffed out the location and were crowding every available flat surface. The director addressed them through a megaphone, begging for silence, while Gavin Graham moved through the crowd eavesdropping on snippets of conversation.

'They say a police helicopter is on the way to pick her up as soon as they wrap.'

'Look at the way she's looking at him now. That's a killer's eyes, that is.'

'Don't be daft. Maggie isn't a killer. I reckon it's that black bloke.'

'That son of hers is a bit black too, isn't he? Got to be one of them.'

'She's killed once, she could kill again.'

It was this final remark that Gavin e-mailed back to Sonia from the cool of the production office – proof, if proof were needed, that the viewing public would believe anything it was told, and made no distinction between truth and fiction, between Eileen and Maggie.

Gavin e-mailed a contact at the *Herald* to tell him that police boats were anchored at the foot of the cliff just in case 'Eileen did it again', then he drove back to the location and looked out contentedly over a calm, blue and utterly vessel-free sea.

The rest of the day went without interruption, as, due to some hasty rewriting, Eileen/Maggie had most of the lines, leaving T. J./Vince to fill in with a few yeahs, nahs and buts. The fatal tussle was filmed a good ten metres from the cliff edge, but with clever use of foreshortening it appeared that Maggie really was pushing her violent lover to his well-deserved death. The director called 'cut' and 'it's a wrap', and Eileen was whisked back to unit base to have her black eye removed.

To everyone's surprise, there was a police car waiting for Eileen when she got back to the hotel, and by the time Danny and Paul were sitting down for a fish supper on the Sliema waterfront Eileen was on a plane to London, accompanied by two British officers.

chapter nine

Those sections of the news media not owned by Six Media had been so loud in their demands for justice that the forces of law and order had little choice but to do something about Eileen Weathers. Questions had even been asked in the House of Commons by an MP who had once been a journalist and had been sacked by Six, and therefore had an axe to grind. Was it right, he asked, that a suspected murderer should be protected from the law just because she was famous? Would the same leniency be extended to any black kid on the streets of, er, Peckham? He thought not. He thought the House should think not. He joined the *Herald* in its demands for justice, and even used the word 'extradition', which went down well.

Once everyone had decided that Eileen Weathers was a killer, and that Jimmy and Gemma were her victims, action was inevitable. Scotland Yard talked to its people in Malta, and Eileen was apprehended 'without a struggle', as the papers reported with some disappointment. She arrived at Heathrow 'under heavy guard', looking every inch the celebrity murderess in big shades and a headscarf. She wasn't cuffed, but she was wearing some chunky silver jewellery around her wrists that was almost as good. She looked, said the papers, 'drawn and haggard'.

Nobody bothered to point out that she wasn't under arrest, that she had just been brought in – rather more flamboyantly than usual – for questioning.

From her eyrie high above the *New Town* lot, Sonia Sutherland observed the frenzy with glee. Viewing figures were rising, despite the fact that the show itself had yet to feature any of her storylines and was still sloshing around in a pre-Sutherland morass of recycling, truancy and prostate trouble. But the signs were good. By sheer publicity alone, there would be an audience big enough to appreciate the shock of the new when it arrived. It couldn't have gone better if Sonia had planned it that way.

And you really have to wonder if she had. Television being such a chaotic affair, good things do sometimes happen by accident – but it would be hard to believe that this was a coincidence. Eileen's notoriety, the arrival of a new executive producer with a point to prove, the urgency of raising the ratings and revenue, the massive press interest that made *New Town* front-page news…Suddenly, the show was required viewing. People talked about it around water coolers, cement mixers and bongs. It was a publicist's dream.

Quite literally: Gavin Graham dreamed the whole thing up while the last embers of the Essex mansion were still smouldering. He knew that there was no greater fame than that of a killer. He saw Eileen at bay, surrounded by the snapping dogs of the press, and he liked what he saw. Everyone involved thought that he was acting exclusively for and with them. Eileen believed that Gavin was 'her' PR man and that everything he did was in her long-term interest. Sonia Sutherland believed that Gavin would exploit Eileen's personal circumstances to boost the show – all to the greater glory of Sonia Sutherland. The *Daily Beacon* (pro-Six) believed that they had 'exclusive' access to all the behind-the-scenes *New Town* stories, which they ran on a daily basis. The *Daily Herald* (anti-Six) believed Gavin was a double agent, appearing to work for the show but feeding the *Herald* with the drip-drip-drip of rumour and suspicion.

But Gavin was working only for himself and took money from the lot of them. He had expenses of his own. Questions in the House don't come cheap.

Everyone struck while the iron was hot, and things moved fast after Eileen's early return from Malta. In one way or another, *New Town* was on the front of every paper, every day, knocking everything else to page two. It was a very good time to bury bad news.

Sonia capitalised on this upsurge of interest by leaking some juicy stories about her plans for the show. Thus it was that several long-serving actors discovered that they were surplus to requirements in the new, slimline, blood-soaked *New Town*. Poppy Ditchling, she revealed, would be mugged and then stabbed by an asylum seeker and found dying by her own husband, Dr Lazarus, who would be unable to save her, despite a lifetime of medical experience. In her last moments she would gasp out the fact that she had been a lesbian for most of their married life and carrying on with a woman in nearby Pease Pottage. 'But you're a pillar of the WI,' Laz would sob through tears as Poppy died in his arms, smiling.

Hayley would have an on-screen mental breakdown when she found out that her own mother was a murderer, and would be sectioned in a gripping scene that would, for the first time, take a no-holds-barred look at the real horror of mental illness. (That took care of Tricia Marvell, whom Sonia regarded with some justification as the worst actress she had ever seen.) Dave Stannard-Watson would follow his wife Dawn, who had left the show in a hurry when Gemma Leeds was killed, and they would start a new life in Manchester. This suited everyone, particularly that photographer in Earl's Court who was now free to publish his 'physique studies' of Steve Seddon wherever he bloody well liked.

Of the original cast, this left only Terri Lee, who was near retirement age, Tim Boreham (whom Sonia intended to turn into a misogynistic serial killer next year), Benjamin Oluwatobi (that voodoo story still had legs), Tyrone D and Leah Wilkinson, both of whom were getting a lot of interest from the teen mags. And so Sonia was free to bring in all her 'mates' from other shows, all of them young, cute and wooden. It didn't matter that this sort of catalogue model would never live in a dump like Eastgate; they looked good on screen, and they would do as they were told.

Eileen's initial questioning by the police was perfunctory. They asked the questions they had asked before, and she gave the same answers. Nobody was getting anywhere with this, and so the case was handed over to Scotland Yard, who were quite prepared to treat it as a full-scale murder inquiry, if that's what the press wanted. They were already under fire for failing to investigate in any thorough way the obvious murders of a handful of black teenagers (one of whom had cut his own windpipe when he fell on a discarded yoghurt pot, according to the 'evidence'); the Weathers case gave the perfect high-profile opportunity to tie up a few loose ends.

Rumour had grown around the corpses of Jimmy and Gemma like toadstools on a log. There were allegations that the bodies had been somehow 'interfered with' before the autopsy, that staff at the hospital had despoiled them for 'gruesome souvenirs' that were now selling for a fortune on eBay. Jimmy's body showed signs of 'violent, possibly deadly' anal abuse, although how this could be established on what amounted to little more than a shovelful of ashes was hard to imagine.

When the press found out that Eileen's right-hand man was 'a self-confessed homosexual' who was having an affair with 'a writer', the die was cast. With such undesirable types at close quarters, it was hardly surprising that murders took place in the Essex mansion. Had these two gays murdered Gemma in a fit of jealousy (they hate women) before sodomising Jimmy Livesey to death and then torching the evidence? Had Jimmy threatened, perhaps, to reveal that Eileen was after all nothing other than an old trannie, thus sealing his horrible fate?

There were so many questions. The *Herald* dealt with them in a mature and responsible way, by running a phone vote (calls cost £1.00). The voting public, thrilled to be involved in such a great new game, decided overwhelmingly in favour of Eileen's guilt.

Paul awoke in bed one night to the sound of footsteps in his flat. By the time he had screamed, got up and switched on the light, the flat was empty – but the door was open. Nothing had been removed or disturbed, but it was enough to frighten him, and he phoned Danny in a panic, saying 'they' had tried to get him. Danny was by Paul's side within an hour, and after a sleepless night Paul had forgotten all about his intruder. The first one, anyway.

The day after *Herald* readers returned their guilty verdict, the Leeds family announced that they were seeking legal advice over the possibility of bringing a private prosecution. The headline said EILEEN WILL STAND TRIAL.

It was at this point that Eileen began to wonder if she'd overplayed her hand.

'They can't say that!' she screamed down the phone to her publicist.

'I'm afraid they can.'

'How the hell did this happen, Gavin? What went wrong?'

Gavin made placatory noises, told her it was 'all good' and reeled off a list of publications desperate for exclusive serial rights to her book (including both the *Beacon* and the *Herald*, whom he was playing off against each other).

'It's not good, darlin',' said Eileen, somewhat calmed by the thought of all that lovely money, 'because as I understand it I could go to prison.'

'It'll never come to that,' said Gavin. 'Nobody's going to come straight out and accuse you of murder. '

The *Herald*'s next front page ran a picture of Eileen under the single word MURDERER. The nation apparently demanded 'justice for Jimmy and Gemma', which had a nice alliterative ring to it. Their tragic mums were united in grief all over pages four and five, and again on seven.

By this time there was open panic in the upper echelons of Channel Six. Although Sonia was experienced enough to know that there's no such thing as adverse publicity, her bean-counting employers had never had much to do with actual programme-making and began to fret about franchise renewal, revenue streams and complaints from the Broadcasting Standards Authority.

Nick Needs called Sonia into his West End office; this hadn't happened to her since she was expelled from her expensive Catholic girls' school.

'I'm worried, Sonia.'

She could see that; his face was the colour of putty, and he seemed to have lost most of his hair.

'What's up?' She knew all too well.

'It's *New Town*…'

'I thought it might be.'

'The thing is, Sonia, what you're doing is obviously brilliant, exactly what we asked you to do, bold and dramatic, engaging ABC1 viewers twenty-five to thirty-five without alienating the core of older, downmarket viewers…'

'Great.'

'But I'm afraid there's a problem.'

Confronted with problems, Sonia had a very special look that turned most antagonists, be they men, women or her own children, to stone. This she turned on Nick, looking up through her super-conditioned chestnut tresses like a well-groomed psychopath. Nick swallowed hard but continued. This was more serious than Sonia thought.

'There's been a lot of press.'

'Yeah, great, isn't it?'

He pulled the *Herald* from a pile on his desk. Tricia Marvell, who used to play Maggie's daughter Hayley until Sonia had sacked her, was pictured wearing a white lace teddy, directing readers to 'pages eight and nine', where she would reveal, among other things, her 'sizzling soap secrets'.

'Oh, that,' sneered Sonia. 'Just another has-been rustling up a few bucks before she hits the panto circuit. Forget it, mate. Tomorrow's fish and chips.'

Nick cleared his throat and read aloud. '"There were always dealers hanging around the lot," says Tricia. "It was so hard to say no. Many of the cast are high on cocaine. The shooting schedule is so intense that it's the only way anyone can keep going."'

'Crap, and you know it.'

'"I made love to Tyrone D when he first joined the show,"' confesses the sexy thirty-eight-year-old. "He was such a great lover, I couldn't believe he was only fourteen. And I wasn't the only one. There were often queues at his dressing room door."'

'Good for him. Little devil…' But Sonia sounded less confident.

'Apart from drug offences and under-age sex,' said Nick, 'we've also had allegations of gross financial misconduct, rigging of viewing figures, intimidation and threats used against family members. That's just in the last week.'

'Come on, it's part of the game, Nick.'

'And you'll notice I haven't even mentioned the Eileen Weathers business.'

'That's out of our hands.'

'Advertisers are pulling out every single day. We're haemorrhaging viewers.'

'We were. We're not now.'

'The BSA has upheld a complaint about the upcoming murder storyline.'

'How can there be a complaint? Nobody's seen it yet.'

'Scripts have been leaked.'

'They're fakes.'

Nick didn't seem to be listening. 'And so I'm afraid my hand is forced.'

Sonia actually felt herself blushing for the first time in over twenty years. 'What do you mean, Nick?'

'I'm going to have to ask you to remove the murder.'

At first Sonia didn't comprehend. 'But a later timeslot would…'

'No, Sonia. Drop it. Write it out. Lose it.'

'I can't do that.'

'You can.'

'You can't make me.'

'Sonia, I hate to do this, because I respect you as a professional and as a woman,' said Nick, staring out of the window at the Soho skyline, 'but I'm very much afraid that I can.'

'I'll walk.'

'Yes, I thought you might say that. And I can't stop you. I would just draw your attention to the penalty clauses in your contract, however.'

'You wouldn't dare.' She gave him the full effect. It had never failed before.

'It's out of my hands,' said Nick with the hint of a smile.

'But this is the biggest chance you've ever had to turn the show into a hit,' said Sonia. If she couldn't intimidate her opponent, she was willing to try the ultimate weapon – reason. '*New Town* has never had such a profile before. Everyone, but everyone, is talking about it. Taxi drivers won't stop going on about it. It's the only show anyone wants to see. They're already talking about the murder, and we haven't even shown Malta yet. It's the biggest thing to happen since Who Shot JR? And you're seriously thinking about throwing all that away?'

'Sonia, we have a responsibility to the audience, to the advertisers and to the shareholders.'

'Exactly! And if you blow this, you'll lose the strongest brand you've got, because *New Town* will never survive.'

'I understand your disappointment, Sonia. I know that you and the team have worked very hard on this project…'

Sonia lost her temper, which was a mistake. 'Don't patronise me, you spineless twat! I've just delivered a piece of fucking classic TV and you're too lily-livered to handle it! You know what, Nick, you and your type are fucking killing British television. You haven't an ounce of drama or passion or creativity in you. You're just a sad little pen-pusher who wouldn't know a good story if it grabbed him by the throat and…' She was at a loss for words. This was a first.

'If you decide to stay with us,' said Nick, rising gloriously above it all, 'I'd like to see a revised episode breakdown on my desk by tomorrow morning.'

'You must be joking.'

'And if you feel you can't stay,' he continued, 'I'll be happy to accept your resignation between now and four o'clock this afternoon. You see, we must make alternative arrangements. So perhaps you could let me know.'

'I'll let you know all right. I'll fucking let you know.'

'Thank you. That's all.'

Sonia retired to lick her wounds and decided, after smoking thirty cigarettes in just over an hour, that she could not afford to leave *New Town* on a bad note: it would look too much like failure. She regretted her behaviour – it was a day of firsts for Sonia – and hoped that Nick Needs would put her temper tantrum down to creative differences. By 3pm she got her secretary to send his secretary a memo announcing that 'Sonia Sutherland will be steering *New Town* through its current difficulties with a raft of exciting new storylines', for all the world as if she was talking to the press.

*

And so *New Town* went right round the S-bend. Without the murder storyline, there was nothing left to show. Half the cast had already been sacked, and the new characters that Sonia had brought in (all those edgy gangster types) had yet to register with viewers.

All she had left were Dr and Mrs Ditchling – and we know her plans for them. Sonia's pen was poised over the letter that would have put 'that old mare' (as she called Marjorie Mayhew) 'out to grass' – but suddenly Sonia realised that without Poppy Ditchling she would have an even bigger hole in her schedules. Instead of sacking Marjorie, she called her in for a chat.

Marjorie, as an old theatrical, had never taken to Sonia and feared the worst.

'I suppose my time has come, and I can't say I'm sorry to go. This is no longer a show I wish to be associated with.'

Sonia swallowed her words, and tried charm. It sounded as if she was speaking a foreign language.

'I just wanted you to know, actually, how much we value you here at *New Town*.'

'My agent will negotiate redundan…What? What did you say?'

'That we value your contribution enormously. You're the heart and soul of the show. I've always said so.'

'You haven't.'

'You provide comedy, compassion, continuity…'

Marjorie hadn't spent all those years in weekly rep without recognising bullshit when she smelled it.

'What do you want?'

'I'm talking to all the core cast members to get their creative input.'

'No, you're not.'

'And I feel that Poppy is very central to…er… the direction in which I see *New Town*…er…going.'

'Is this a Gotcha?' Marjorie looked around the office for cameras.

'So if you have any ideas for how we might take her forward…' The truth was that Sonia didn't have a clue about Poppy's storylines, so sure had she been of cutting the character. 'I mean, in your own words, what's her story arc over the next six months?'

'Well,' said Marjorie, 'of course she's just discovered that her thyroid is overactive. Or is it underactive?'

'Right. A major concern for our viewers.'

'So she'll be very hyperactive…or is it sluggish? I can never remember. Which one gives you the bulging eyes and the goitre?'

'OK, we'll get research on to it.'

'And what with Laz's prostate trouble…'

'Hmm,' said Sonia, pacing. 'Glands. Glands. Glands. Is it possible to do a thryoid transplant?'

'I don't think so, dear, but a friend of mine's just had an operation.'

'Or would they form a suicide pact…?'

'It's not life threatening.'

'But isn't it? And why have they both got it now?'

'It's their age, dear.'

'No. It's something more than that. It's the overflow from a nuclear waste processing plant, covered up by the government, that's been built near Eastgate. Are the kiddies at risk? I'm thinking mutant births.'

'Oh, Sonia,' said Marjorie, 'you really are a ridiculous woman.' She gathered herself up and left.

Over the next few weeks, however, Marjorie was obliged to work harder than she had ever worked in her life, even during that memorable season at Guildford when she had played Saint Joan, Mrs Malaprop and Blanche DuBois on alternate days for six whole weeks. Poppy's thyroid became the most famous gland in the history of television, its daily ups and downs setting the pace for the nation's least successful drama. One day she'd be zipping around the Eastgate shops as if on speed, lending credence to claims that the entire cast were coke fiends. Then, without warning, she'd be seen expiring on a couch, a quiet, valedictory figure around whom mourning groups would spontaneously form. Letters poured in to the *New Town* offices claiming that 'yo-yo thyroid' was a condition so far unknown to medical science, but Sonia didn't care. For the time being it was all she had to work on.

She would dearly love to have promoted Dr Lazarus's prostate to equal glory, sharing the billing, as it were, but when she proposed that storyline to Channel Six she was told that it was 'too explicit for prime time'. And so Poppy's thyroid had to carry the whole weight of a four-nights-a-week soap by itself.

You can stretch a thyroid only so far, and within a couple of weeks the viewing figures, already seriously compromised by the events of the last six months, had dipped to an all-time low. *New Town* was not only being beaten in the ratings by every other soap the competition had to offer – it was even struggling against serious documentaries, current affairs and religious programmes. On one memorable evening, viewers plumped for a re-run of *How Clean Is Your Pyramid?* rather than face another half-hour of Poppy's bulging eyes and swollen neck.

Sonia watched the ratings plunge with admirable sangfroid. She knew that, sooner or later, something had to give.

And what of Eileen? Her character was, the viewers knew, 'on holiday'. Most single mothers who work in launderettes would find it difficult to afford a month in the sun – not Maggie, however, who failed to return week after week. Nobody in Eastgate mentioned her, or Vince or Dean or Bernard – it was as if they had suddenly ceased to exist. Their screen families, what was left of them, didn't even get postcards.

But if Maggie was in some kind of Mediterranean limbo, Eileen herself was in real-life hell. She didn't know whether she had a job or not; every time she tried to phone Sonia or Nick to discuss her return to the show, she was put through to voicemail. If she managed to track one of them down they were suddenly surrounded by production secretaries who formed a barrier between talent and employer. It didn't take Eileen long to realise that she was, to all intents and purposes, suspended from the show. Worse still, there was the unfinished business of helping the police with their inquiries. She cooperated fully, turning up on time, answering questions frankly, leaving at the end of each ghastly session exhausted, humiliated but uncharged. Then another story would appear in the press, another allegation that Eileen had hired a hitman, or fiddled with the wiring, and she would be called back to the station once again.

In between times, she poured out her life story to Paul. Their meetings went from three times a week to four, to five, finally to six. He was spending more time at Eileen's temporary home in Kensington than he was in his own flat in Waterloo; he even had his own guest bed there. The tone of the book changed suddenly from one of light, je-ne-regrette-rien anecdotal banter to something altogether darker. Eileen spoke with relish of her involvement in a handful of nasty 1960s gangland slayings. She was harsh in her judgement of colleagues – and this wasn't just frivolous gossip. She suddenly remembered every bastard who'd done her down, stolen her jobs, stolen her boyfriends or otherwise stood in her way. All of this was music to Paul's ears – he was learning the value of scandal – but he began to worry for Eileen's sanity. She lost weight, her roots began to grow out and she was smoking and drinking more than was good for her. One vodka and tonic led to another, and frequently she had to lie down in the afternoons, leaving Paul alone to transcribe his tapes, accompanied by the rhythm of her snoring.

Danny, who could have helped him to while away the hours, was nowhere to be seen. Officially, he was overseeing the rebuilding of the Essex mansion (and Paul had indeed received a few welcome visits from him, still unwashed from the site). But Paul began to wonder if Danny needed him as much as he once had.

Both Eileen and Sonia were surprised, to say the least, when they picked up the *Daily Beacon* one morning to learn that '*New Town* bosses' had decided in 'a surprise move' to run the 'controversial murder storyline' filmed several weeks ago in Malta.

Within moments, the Six switchboard was going into meltdown. Nick Needs's mobile wasn't answering. Gavin Graham was nowhere to be found. Sonia got hold of Eileen just as Eileen was trying to get hold of Sonia.

'Well?'

'Well what?'

'What the fuck are you playing at?'

'What the fuck are *you* playing at?'

There was a pause, then they both spoke together.

'Have you seen today's…?'

'It says in today's…'

And so, for a while, the two women were friends, or at least allies in adversity. They raged against the incompetence and dishonesty of their male employers and co-workers. They ranted about the portrayal of 'tough' women by a sexist media. Eventually they got round to agreeing that, if 'they' were really going to run with the murder storyline, they would have to pay through the nose for it. They weren't quite clear what they meant by this, but it sounded good and made them feel a lot better.

While Eileen and Sonia were bonding, Nick Needs had finally plucked up the courage to ring them both and left a message inviting them to a meeting the following afternoon. He did not tell them just how close the axe had come to falling on *New Town*. He did not mention the emergency meeting with Channel Six's controller, who told him, in no uncertain terms, that if *New Town* did not return to 'viable audience mass' within a month, he would have no option but to close it down. If Nick had anything up his sleeve, said the controller, now was the time to pull it out.

And so *New Town* was reborn.

Instead of the washed-out tones of Eastgate, of Poppy's pale mottled flesh and the grey skies of an English winter, suddenly on to the screen burst the intense blue of a Mediterranean sky, the harsh chromium yellow of Maltese sandstone, the brown sheen of warm, tanned skin. It was the soap equivalent of Dorothy's emergence into Munchkinland.

Over a week of mounting excitement, during which the show ran every night and twice on Friday, the nation was glued to the long-anticipated build-up to the murder of Vince the window-cleaner. They watched as Maggie and Vince tried to rekindle the spark of their romance over a series of increasingly passionate lunches and dinners. They chewed their lips off as Vince turned nasty and punched Maggie in the gut, causing her to puke her red snapper over the harbour wall. They gasped as Bernard turned up out of the blue, his eyes ablaze with murderous voodoo intent. They panted as Dean frolicked in his Speedos, then wept as he swore to avenge his mother's sufferings.

And then it all ended up on that lonely clifftop high above the glittering waves of the southern Med, where Vince watched with dumb shock as his killer came cannoning towards him, impacted with his stomach and sent him bouncing down the cliff face to a foamy death.

As the waves washed over his lifeless corpse, and the surf turned pink with his blood, the credits rolled in silence. Moments like this were just too good to be ruined by the show's hideous theme tune.

The whodunnit aspect of the murder storyline was a bit of a joke, as the world and his wife already knew that there was only one killer in *New Town*, and Eileen, sorry, Maggie was her name. The climactic week ended with a supposed cliffhanger, as the identity of the killer had not yet been revealed – but there was little doubt in anyone's mind that she had done it again.

The following week, the papers reported *New Town*'s highest viewing figures since the legendary wedding of 1979. Sonia and Eileen were snapped arriving at a premiere, all smiles.

On the Tuesday, *New Town* viewers learned that their suspicions were correct, as they watched Maggie reliving the murder from her point of view. By the end of the week, the Eastgate police had swung into action, and the estate was crawling with cops.

On the Friday, after a gruelling episode in which Maggie almost cracked under interrogation by Rooksfield CID, the ratings broke the 1979 record. Nick Needs started talking about the Baftas.

And Eileen Weathers received a letter informing her that a private prosecution relating to the deaths of Jimmy Livesey and Gemma Leeds would require her presence in court in two weeks' time.

On the Monday, Eileen was once again summoned to Harlow police station, where she was interviewed, charged with murder and remanded in custody.

chapter ten

It didn't take long to arrange bail; Gavin Graham saw to that, with a hefty down payment from one of the papers in return for exclusives to come. So Eileen spent only one night in custody, which doesn't exactly amount to a 'jail hell' but made for a great headline on her release.

At the end of the week, Paul received a call from one of his fair-Weathers friends.

'Well, you must be very disappointed.'

'Why?'

'Haven't you read the paper this morning?'

'No, I'm too busy working on this book.'

'I'd save your energies if I were you.'

Paul ran to the news-stand and learned, to his surprise, that '*New Town* star Eileen Weathers's controversial autobiography has been "indefinitely postponed" by publisher Six Books pending the outcome of her forthcoming trial for the murder of Jimmy Livesey and Gemma Leeds'.

He left messages on Emma and Toby's voicemail at Six Books, stressing the urgency of his call, and waited for a response that never came.

The following day he received this e-mail:

From: Toby Ross, editorial director, Six Books
Re: Eileen Weathers

Dear Paul

Thanks very much for all your hard work on Eileen Weathers's autobiography. At this time we are revising our lists and looking at a slight reschedule of the publication date.

Please don't hesitate to contact us with any new ideas, and we wish you all the best of luck for the future.

Toby

Paul finally got through on the telephone; someone forgot to tell the temp not to connect his calls.

'Toby, it's Paul Mackrell.'

'Paul…Thing is, I'm in a meeting.'

'Just tell me exactly when you intend to publish Eileen's book.'

'We're just looking over the legal position, and we think…'

'You're dropping it, aren't you?'

'Given the sensitive nature of the material, I realise now we should have hired a more experienced writer.'

'You're pulling the plug on the best-selling title you're ever likely to publish.'

'But under the circumstances,' said Toby, 'we're prepared to be generous.'

'Listen to me! You can't drop the book now!'

'If you read the contract…'

'OK,' said Paul. 'We'll take the book to someone with the guts to do it.'

The tone of Toby's voice changed from one of false mateyness to something even less appealing. 'Of course, all the material is wholly owned by Six Books.'

'What material? I haven't delivered anything.'

'Yes…a few chapters, I understand.'

'Rough drafts,' said Paul. 'Not finished.'

'And obviously if we're to release the remaining payments due on your contract, we would need you to hand over all working materials, research notes, drafts and transcripts.'

'Never.'

'And if you're unable to do so…' Paul heard the rustling of paper. 'Then the £6,000-plus still owed on your advance would remain with our accounts department while we pursue the return of our property. It's all outlined in the contract, Paul.'

Paul thought of the stress and expense of a lawsuit. He thought of all the writing time that £6,000 could buy him. He thought of Eileen's erratic, secretive behaviour since the fire – not to mention Danny's apparent desertion.

Was it worth gambling £6,000 on such an uncertain prospect?

Toby sensed victory. 'Thing is, Paul,' he said, 'publishing is about the brand. When we signed the deal, the Eileen Weathers brand was hot. Now it's not.'

'But the story,' said Paul weakly. 'The story is fantastic.'

'It could be the greatest story ever told, mate, and it wouldn't move off the bookshelves. The buyers don't like what she's done, and we can't afford to piss off the buyers.'

'But the writing? The writing's good…'

'Writing's great, Paul. We love writing. But at Six Books we don't do writing. We do brands.'

If he had been a character in one of the coming-of-age novels that he forced his students to read, Paul would at this point have embarked on a picaresque odyssey through the lower depths of London's underworld. He was, after all, disillusioned, broken-hearted and comparatively rich. His advance would have seemed like thirty pieces of silver, the price of his betrayal of Eileen, and he would have spent it on cheap drugs and cheaper sex.

Unlike those characters, however, Paul actually needed the money, being without private income, and he was by nature a cautious soul. This does not make for prize-winning fiction, but did at least enable him to meet his mortgage payments.

Eileen called him a few days after her arrest, requesting a meeting at a favourite restaurant behind the Brompton Oratory, just a short stagger from her temporary Kensington home. When Paul arrived at 12.30pm, she was already several aperitifs ahead of him. She was speaking – or rather shouting – on her phone to someone that Paul guessed was her agent.

'What do you mean, there's nothing you can do?' she said, motioning Paul to sit, dropping ash in her vodka and tonic as she did so. 'What do you think I'm paying you for, you stupid cow?'

Paul sat rigid in his chair as waiters hovered. He ordered a bottle of mineral water and wished the ground would swallow him up.

'Contract? I don't care about the fucking contract, darlin'! That's your job, isn't it? I'm writing the bloody thing. It's my book, it's my life, and they can't just…WHAT DO YOU MEAN THEY CAN? Oh, well, if that's your attitude you can go FUCK YOURSELF!'

She threw the phone back into her handbag.

'The bitch says it's my fault the contract's void because there was a fucking morals clause about bringing Six Media into disrepute. Morals? They wouldn't know fucking morals if they…if they…' She drank deep. Paul was trembling at the prospect of telling her that he'd pulled out of their collaboration, bought off by £6,000.

'We'll sue the bastards, that's what we'll do.'

'I'm not sure if we can…'

'I'm not taking this lying down,' she said, gesturing away the waiter who had come to take a food order. Paul was hungry, but food was not on the agenda. 'I'm a powerful woman. I have friends.'

This was exactly what Paul did not want to hear; Eileen's 'friends' had already got her into plenty of hot water, if the papers were to be believed.

'But Eileen,' he said, determined to sober her up, 'you're already suing *New Town*.'

'Yeah…Well they've dropped me. I haven't done anything to deserve it.'

'And there's that libel suit against the *Herald*.'

'They can't get away with printing those lies.'

'And the one against the *Beacon*.'

'They're just as bad.'

'And you're suing the builders who are working on the Essex mansion.'

'Are you trying to tell me how to run my life, darlin'?' said Eileen, turning bloodshot eyes on Paul.

'Not at all. I'm just concerned about where the money's coming from. Lawyers are expensive.'

'Don't worry about me, Paul,' said Eileen, fumbling with an empty cigarette packet. 'I don't need bloody lawyers. I'm representing myself.'

While she stormed off to buy fags, Paul backed out of the smoke-filled room and made his way sadly back to Waterloo.

And that, thought Paul, was that. He retired from the fray, battered but otherwise intact, with enough material for at least two novels. He would live frugallly on £6,000, withdraw from the shallow social whirl and write.

Two days later, he was summoned back to the same restaurant.

'It's OK,' Eileen laughed on the phone. 'I won't get pissed this time. I have a proposition to make. The car will pick you up at 12.30. Just bring a notebook.'

She was at the bar waiting for him, sipping water and looking better groomed than he had seen her in weeks. She kissed him warmly on both cheeks, which impressed the staff.

'Paul, darlin',' she said, 'you look fabulous. Thanks for coming.'

Paul sensed that he was about to be seduced.

'I won't beat about the bush,' she said, when they were seated at a discreet table away from prying eyes. 'I want to put a bit of business your way.'

'Yes?'

'Tell me in all honesty: do you think my story's any good?'

'Of course I do.'

'Do you think another publisher would go for it?'

'Yes, but…'

'But we're bound by contracts with Six Books, who have bought off all your drafts and your research material. I know.'

Paul blushed and fiddled with his starter.

'I don't blame you, darlin'. A boy has to live.'

'So what are you suggesting?'

'Something new. Something really radical,' she said, crunching a mouthful of rocket. Her eyes were twinkling.

'And what's that?' For a moment Paul feared a self-help book.

'The truth.'

Paul whistled.

'That surprised you, didn't it? The truth, the whole truth and nothing but the ugly, unvarnished truth. All the stuff I didn't tell you before. All the stuff I've tried to hush up over the years. How about it? The real deal.'

'You mean what you told me before was—'

'Lies? Not all of it, no. But there's nothing in there that's so very important. Nothing that matters.'

Paul felt a chasm opening in the centre of the table, and inside, swarming from the depths, were all those long-suppressed truths from Eileen's past. His head whirled.

'The truth,' he said. 'The real truth this time?'

'Yeah, why not,' said Eileen, pushing her salad away and lighting a cigarette. 'It would certainly be original, wouldn't it?'

'But so dangerous. I mean, the legal implications alone…'

'Libel, you mean?' said Eileen. 'Don't worry about that. They can't sue if it's true.'

Paul wondered who had been coaching Eileen in defamation law.

'It's risky, though.'

'For me, maybe. Not for you. I want you to provide a service. Just do what you do, make me talk, get it down and turn it into words on paper. You'll be well paid, darlin', and there your responsibility ends. Leave the rest of it to me. I'll sell it, and I'll face the consequences.'

'But you're already involved in all those other legal actions.'

'Dropped 'em, darlin'. Went a bit mad for a moment, didn't I? Don't worry, it's in the past. You have to allow us artists to show a bit of temperament from time to time. Now I've finished sulking and I'm ready to fight the bastards at their own game.'

'Well, if you're sure…'

'I knew I could trust you, Paul.'

'When do we start?'

'This afternoon, darlin'. I've got deadlines to meet.'

*

The following week the *Daily Herald* ran the first of its exclusive extracts from Eileen Weathers's autobiography, *Men, Marriage and Me*. In it, she spoke frankly of her relationship with her father, Edward Gutteridge – no longer the distant, shadowy fish salesman of her previous efforts, but a vicious, philandering alcoholic who made his family's life a misery, who beat his wife and even diddled his own daughters. He had families up and down the 68 bus route, moving between them as necessity demanded. When Eileen's mother kicked him out of the Elephant and Castle, he drifted south to Camberwell, thence to Herne Hill, finally to West Norwood, the furthest he had cast his seed. Then back to the Elephant, remorseful and broke, to renew the cycle. Christmas Day was Edward Gutteridge's worst nightmare.

Another day, another drama – and in part two Eileen spoke openly of her loveless marriage to *New Town* star Charlie Weathers, a much older man with the sexual appetite of a depraved goat. 'I was so trusting, so full of hope, and so flattered to be wined and dined by a star of Charlie's magnitude,' gushed Eileen in Paul's most heated prose. 'But I soon realised that marriage to Charlie was one long round of disappointments. No sooner was the ring on my finger than he was off with one starlet after another – some of them now the biggest names in British show business!'

After further extracts dealing with her painful divorce, her string of affairs with athletic young working-class men, many of them boxers, and her second marriage to Essex builder and millionaire Brian Champion ('long downstairs but thick upstairs'), the *Herald*'s readers were eating out of Eileen's hand. They loved her for her frankness, her vulnerability and her self-deprecating humour. 'I've been a silly cow, I know,' she said at the end of one particularly effective instalment, 'but whatever I've done, whatever mistakes I've made in a long and eventful life have all been for the best possible reason. And that reason has always been love.'

The *Herald*'s sales figures soared, as readers who had traditionally been put off by the paper's anti-*New Town* editorial stance finally got the chance to revel in an orgy of tittle-tattle.

Public opinion was revolutionised. Eileen was a lover, a fighter, a survivor. But she was no longer – how could she be? – a killer.

In restaurants and at book fairs, Eileen's memoirs rapidly became the subject of an intense bidding war between rival publishers. Six Books held themselves above the fray, and Toby Ross lost his job.

Day after day, Eileen's confessional commanded front pages around the world.

'Eileen,' said Paul during interviews one morning, 'we really can't put this in.'

'What?'

'"He regularly entertained his coke-dealer boyfriend in the *New Town* dressing room."'

'But it's true. Justification!' This was Eileen's favourite new word.

'You'll be sued.'

'Listen, darlin', if that old queen Terri Lee is prepared to dig into his sordid past, he's more stupid than I thought. Besides which, he can't afford legal action, because he's tight as arseholes. And besides all that, it's God's honest truth.'

'But it's so…sordid.'

'That's nothing, darlin'. The story goes that the dealer in question was soon providing his services to the upper echelons of the Channel Six management, some of whom paid him to blow coke up their arseholes. But I ain't put that in, have I,' said Eileen with a saintly expression, 'because I wouldn't want to make waves.'

And so she laid waste her former co-stars, her employers, her husbands and her lovers. When she started in on her affair with Jimmy Livesey, the *Herald*'s sales figures burst all records. 'I was addicted to just one thing – his lovemaking,' wrote Paul. 'It was a classic May-to-September romance. I had the experience, he had the energy. Together we were dynamite – and dangerous.'

Her struggles to keep the marriage going, to maintain Jimmy's interest as the crow's feet and varicose veins set in, were guaranteed to win over the *Herald*'s largely female readership. Secure the hearts of the nation's menopausal millions, Eileen knew, and no jury would dare convict her.

*

While Eileen was making her pre-emptive strike through the pages of the *Daily Herald*, the police were preparing evidence for the forthcoming trial. Scotland Yard left no stone unturned in their search for the truth. Compared with the previous investigation, which had been heavily criticised in the press, this was ruthless. Everyone with a connection to Eileen and Jimmy was called in and treated as if they personally had started the fire.

The day before Paul was due to be interviewed, Danny turned up at his house. It was the first time Paul had seen him in weeks; officially he'd been overseeing the rebuilding of the Essex mansion, but Paul knew in his heart that Danny had other fish to fry and that their affair had fizzled out. This did not come as a surprise – how could Paul ever hope to hold a man like Danny? – but that didn't make the parting any easier.

And now, suddenly, here was Danny on his doorstep, fresh from the building site, his tanned, muscular arms lightly dusted with plaster, his old jeans spattered with paint.

'Come in,' said Paul, who planned to be slightly frosty. 'You'd better take your boots off.'

'I'd better take everything off,' said Danny.

An hour later, Paul's frostiness had thawed, and he lay exhausted on the sofa.

'Where have you been, Danny?'

'You know where I've been, Paolo. Working on Lady Muck's bloody house. I don't know why she didn't just bulldoze the place and start from scratch.'

'But you never returned my calls…'

'They told me not to.'

'Who…they?'

'Them bastards at Channel Six. Told me not to see you no more, made it look bad for Eileen. All that stuff in the papers, mate, "Eileen's Pal's Gay Love Shame".'

'What's Channel Six got to do with anything? They've dropped her from the show.'

'She's still on the payroll, mate. Ah, didn't tell you that, did she? So whatever Channel Six wants, Channel Six gets.'

'So what you really mean is that Eileen told you not to see me.'

'Paolo, mate, don't be hard on her. She's had a shit time. Prison was very hard for her.'

'Prison? She was only in police custody for one night.'

'But this is a lady who's used to getting her own way. Who knows what they did to her in there? You know what those WPCs are like.'

Paul's head was spinning. 'I need a drink.'

'Not so fast, lover boy.' Danny kissed him again, and this particular disagreement was quickly forgotten.

'So,' said Danny, emerging later from the shower, 'have they called you in for an interview?'

'You know they have. It's tomorrow.'

'Oh, right! I didn't know that.' Danny looked him straight in the eye and carried on towelling his back. He was in no hurry to get dressed.

'Yes, and to be honest I'm very nervous about it.'

'You've got nothing to worry about, Paul. You were with me.'

'I know where I was…'

'And you can't have forgotten what we were doing…' Danny was less than a yard away from him, and Paul could feel the heat beating off his body.

'I know, I know. But I just hate the idea that they could twist that into some kind of lie.'

'Hey,' said Danny, slipping an arm around Paul's shoulders, 'you'll be fine. Just fine.' He kissed him on the mouth. 'Anyway, those coppers aren't so frightening. Just think of it as a friendly chat.'

'Have you been in already, then?'

'Me?' laughed Danny. 'I was the first on the list. Yeah, they tried to make out all sorts of crap, like I was Eileen's boyfriend and I was trying to cover up for her and stuff.'

Paul felt a cold hand on his heart.

'You're not, are you?'

Danny looked him straight in the eye again. 'Paul, one thing you can be sure of, and I swear this on my mother's life, I am not Eileen's boyfriend.'

An hour later, Danny finally got dressed and left the flat.

When Paul turned up at Scotland Yard, all he could think of was the great injustice that had been done to Eileen Weathers, the ridiculous suspicion that had fallen on Danny and the craven behaviour of Channel Six in trying simultaneously to punish and control their biggest star. Now he understood Eileen's anger – the desire for revenge that had pushed her to such painful, self-lacerating confessions in the pages of the *Daily Herald*. With the armies of falsehood ranked so mightily against her, she had just one weapon – the truth.

Paul, of course, was enlisted on her side, and despite the wicked insinuations of the investigating officer he stuck doggedly to the truth.

'So you and Mr Danny Attard were together on the afternoon of the fire,' asked DS King, a silver-haired man of about forty-five whom Paul struggled not to fancy.

'Yes, we were.'

'And how can you be so sure of that?'

'It was a very memorable afternoon.'

'In what sense, Mr Mackrell?'

'Danny and I were lovers.' He looked DS King straight in the eye, searching for some flicker of disgust.

'I see. And you spent the entire afternoon…'

'Yes. The entire afternoon.' In fact, they had spent some of the afternoon sleeping, but DS King didn't need to know that.

'And when you left it was about – what time?'

'Quarter past six. He drove me to the station just in time to get the 18.34 back to London.'

'How can you be so sure?'

'I keep a diary. I'm a writer.'

DS King sighed; yet another alibi was all too depressingly watertight.

'And yet you were at that time in the employment of Miss Weathers, weren't you?'

'No,' said Paul, as if he were explaining to a six-year-old. 'I was being paid by Six Books, a subsidiary of Six Media.'

'But your livelihood depended on your friendship with Miss Weathers.'

'Not particularly. I'm self-employed. I have several strings to my bow.'

'But this was an important job. A job you didn't want to lose.'

'Are you suggesting, Detective Sergeant King, that I'm bending the truth in some way in order to protect Miss Weathers?'

'Or those close to her.'

Paul felt a hormonal rush; he was being called on to defend Danny. He opted for the ice queen approach.

'Do you have any more questions?'

'Yes. Did you ever hear Eileen Weathers talk about killing her husband?'

'No.'

'Can you prove that?'

'You can retrieve the tapes of all our conversations from Six Books.'

'We've already done that.'

'Then I imagine they will provide an answer to that question.'

'What about in your private conversations?'

'Detective Sergeant King,' said Paul grandly, 'I don't know how you imagine the working relationship between an actor and a writer, but let me assure you that Miss Weathers and I did not sit around discussing ways to bump off her husband. Our conversations rarely extended beyond the job that we were both being paid to do. Perhaps we talked about the show, or the dogs, or the house, but she most certainly did not discuss murder.'

'How would you describe her relationship with Mr Livesey?'

Paul realised that honesty was the best policy. 'Terrible.'

'Oh, yes?'

'They bickered all the time. They had blazing rows. In short, it was like any marriage.'

DS King looked down and, Paul thought, blushed. He knew from television dramas that most detective sergeants have disastrous marriages.

'She never threatened him?'

'Look,' said Paul, 'we're talking about an actress here. A soap actress. I've worked with lots of actresses,' he lied, 'and they're just not the type to commit murder. They're too disorganised and self-absorbed. And Eileen Weathers is one of the worst.' She deserved that for having told Danny to keep away from Paul.

'She has friends in the criminal underworld, I understand,' said DS King.

'That's been massively overplayed, not least by Eileen herself. She knocked around with a few second-rate south London gangsters in the '60s and early '70s, but even then I don't think you could have called her dangerous.'

'Were there any suspicious phone calls? Any visitors that you didn't recognise?'

'No,' said Paul. 'She kept herself very private. There were journalists and photographers around, of course, because she was going through problems in her married life.'

'Mr Livesey had moved out, I understand.'

'Well, he was sleeping with his girlfriend.'

'Miss Leeds.'

'Correct. But he still had keys to the house; it was still his home, and he had a lot of his stuff there. Eileen said he'd be back sooner or later. I think it had happened before.'

'But this time it was serious, wasn't it?'

'Not particularly.'

'She'd been publicly humiliated.'

'Oh, DS King,' said Paul, leaning forward and catching a whiff of aftershave, 'Eileen's had worse troubles than that. And she didn't murder any of her former husbands, to the best of my knowledge.'

'Thank you, Mr Mackrell,' said DS King, backing away. 'That will be all…for now.'

And so the iron entered Eileen Weathers's soul. Arrested, widowed, homeless, charged with the murder of her husband and his lover, suspended from her job, dropped by her publisher and temporarily homeless, her private life a tabloid sensation, she was in every sense at bay. Lesser mortals might have buckled under the pressure, but not Eileen Weathers. She looked around her, saw she had nothing left to lose and recognised in that interesting situation not so much a defeat as an opportunity.

The entertainment business abhors a vacuum even more than nature does, and so into the abyss of Eileen's private and professional life there was a sudden rush of offers. A book deal came quickly, from a publisher less timid and less scrupulous than Six Books; she never disclosed the amount of the advance to Paul who, after all, she was paying well for his work. He didn't ask questions; he didn't want his name on the cover, nor anywhere near so potentially defamatory a book.

Agents were sniffing around what was left of her acting career; she'd sacked the last one, who had failed in negotiations with Channel Six and left Eileen high and dry, and let it be known that she was currently unrepresented. Polite interest turned into a mad scramble after the shock announcement that *New Town* was nominated for a Bafta award in the best continuing drama category, and that Eileen herself was in the running for best actress. There were red faces at Channel Six when the news broke, and much talk of bridge-building, but when Nick Needs phoned Eileen she simply told him that, with the forthcoming trial, she had too much on her plate to consider returning to the show in the immediate future. She did, however, remind him that she was getting a number of offers from other channels which, after her shoddy treatment by *New Town*, she was considering very seriously.

Paul was her mainstay through all this, or at least that was the impression she gave him. When the Essex mansion was once again habitable, she let it be known that one of the guest rooms was now 'Paul's room', to use as he pleased. She often asked him to stay for dinner, or breakfast, and although there was obviously never going to be any kind of sexual relationship between them, Paul enjoyed the frisson of being 'the mystery man at Eileen Weathers's side'. Danny, who was still supervising a team of builders, was in and out of the house, in and out of Paul's room and in and out of Paul on a regular basis. The happy little ménage had returned, almost, to the carefree life of old.

Almost, that is, except for the lengthening shadow of the trial. Eileen's legal team were confident that she would get off, that the prosecution's case was so flimsy that the judge would most likely throw it out of court with some stern remarks about wasting time and money. Even so, it was hard for Eileen to relax. Thanks to the constant support of her 'boys', as she liked to call them, she kept her drinking to a minimum, cut down on the fags and spent a good deal of time in her newly installed home gym, built in the shell of what had once been Jimmy's 'den'. She worked hard on the book, she spent many a lunchtime negotiating with agents and producers and was frequently entertained by the increasingly desperate producers of *New Town*. As the odds on Eileen's Bafta victory shortened, their gestures of reconciliation became frankly desperate. Scripts arrived almost every day from *New Town*'s Bromley HQ – scripts that any other soap actress would have killed for. There were storylines that paired her with the actor of her choice; they were talking to some very big American names, they said, as guest stars. There was even talk of an *'Audience with…'* style show, in which Eileen would display her range in front of a studio full of fawning C-list guests. But she held herself above it all.

'Let them come and talk to me when I walk free from that courtroom,' she said. 'Until then, everything is on hold.'

chapter eleven

The prosecution case hinged on a piece of fresh evidence that had not formed part of Eileen's master plan. Calls from her mobile had been traced to an unsavoury south London lowlife called Pat O'Connor, a minor gangster who had done bits of work for Eileen's father. The jury lapped it up; it was just the kind of stuff they enjoyed on television.

Pat O'Connor was singing like a cockney sparrow, a role in which he had been carefully coached. The gallery was full for his performances: colleagues from *New Town* who had taken the day off, the good and the great of the TV world, members of Jimmy and Gemma's families (still united in grief) and as many weird *New Town* fans as could get in. Paul sat unobtrusively at the back, taking notes for the book.

Eileen, claimed Pat O'Connor, had contacted him to 'call in a few favours' and, during the course of several clandestine conversations, let it be known that she wanted to arrange a fire in the Essex mansion. Pat assumed it was an insurance job; back in his day, he was known as Pat the Firestarter O'Connor, or just Zippo. Did this request not strike you as unusual, asked Eileen's brief. No, said O'Connor; he did this sort of thing for a living. He complained that the bottom had fallen out of the arson business, which raised a laugh.

Had Eileen ever mentioned killing her husband? Not in so many words, said O'Connor, but her 'people' had given him to understand that she wouldn't be too heartbroken if Mr Livesey was to 'disappear'.

'Are any of these "people" in the courtroom today?' asked the defence.

O'Connor thought that he recognised a couple of people, but they turned out to be *New Town* stars, whom everyone knew from the telly.

'And you understood this as a contract for murder?'

'Yes, I did,' wheezed O'Connor, a lifelong smoker.

'Didn't it seem rather vague?'

'Oh, no, sir.' O'Connor knew when to wheedle. 'You see, there's very few will come right out and say it. You have to put two and two together.'

'And in this case you arrived at the conclusion that Mrs Livesey wanted her husband to be burned to death with his mistress?'

'No,' laughed O'Connor. 'There was never any mention of the little lady. That was an accident.'

There was a gasp from the public gallery, the journalists had their headline for the morning edition, and the judge concluded the day's business so that they could go and file their copy.

O'Connor's testimony continued the next day. He described in detail how he had soaked the furniture with paraffin, blocking ventilation systems and disabling smoke alarms. He described his sabotage of the wiring at the back of Jimmy's state-of-the-art home cinema, causing it to spark when the TV was switched on.

'It was just a question of time,' he concluded. 'Nobody could have walked out of there alive.' O'Connor had done his job well: forensics couldn't find enough evidence to construct the flimsiest of rebuttals.

It sounded convincing – and, more to the point, the jury finally had someone on whom to pin their long-cherished suspicions about Eileen Weathers and her dodgy gangland connections. The wailing of the Leeds family as they relived the casual, accidental death of their beloved daughter Gemma was the perfect sound effect. Eileen sat impassive throughout; even Paul had trouble figuring out who was telling the truth.

Eileen's testimony was rock solid, delivered with humility and dignity, and failed to make much impression. No, she had never heard of Pat O'Connor, let alone spoken to him. No, she had not wanted her husband dead, nor had she arranged for the house to be burned down in order to get the insurance money. Yes, she had argued with Jimmy, and with Gemma, and yes, she was very upset by their blatant adultery, but no, she had not planned any kind of revenge. She could account for her actions before, during and after the fire; most of them were on film in the *New Town* production office.

'I suggest, Miss Weathers,' said the counsel for the prosecution, a big fruity character with the nose of an incipient alcoholic, 'that you paid several people a great deal of money to arrange for the disposal of your husband. That you were deliberately vague in your orders, leaving Mr O'Connor to understand that he would be handsomely rewarded for a job you knew only too well he would carry out. You left the dirty work to your employees…'

'I have no employees,' interrupted Eileen, 'and as far as I'm aware nobody else is being prosecuted for conspiracy.'

This was partly true; she had Danny, of course, who kept as far from the courtroom as possible, but he had not even been called as a witness. His alibi was watertight. Paul had seen to that.

The trial rumbled on, as witness after unreliable witness repeated stories already familiar from the press about mutilated corpses and sexual shenanigans. None of it had anything to do with the case in hand, but it added to a growing picture of Eileen as an all-round beast. In the end, the fact that her guilt hinged entirely on the testimony of one elderly stool pigeon was buried under a mountain of circumstantial evidence.

In summing up, the judge described Eileen as 'devious, manipulative, a consummate actress' who had been 'evasive at best' in her evidence. In fact, she had answered every question clearly and concisely, but everyone had forgotten this in the light of more sensational material. The jury reached a guilty verdict long before the judge's summing-up.

They were out for a full day, partly because the sandwiches were nice, but also because there was one obstructive juror who did not read tabloid newspapers but who had once read a book about the criminal justice system, He therefore had a basic understanding of such troublesome concepts as 'evidence' and 'guilt', and tried to argue his point. In the end, however, he was browbeaten by the hysterical reaction of his peers and decided, on balance, that Eileen probably did it.

The foreman's voice as he delivered the guilty verdict was almost drowned by ululations from the gallery. The Leeds and Livesey womenfolk had got justice at last, and expressed it in banshee howls that they had learned from television. Had they not been restrained, they would have swarmed to the dock and dismembered Eileen, a pack of maenads in tracksuits.

Of course, the papers were full of Eileen's guilt, although it was hardly news to anyone who had taken the slightest interest in the trial. It was a foregone conclusion that Eileen would go down. People had died, a famous rich person was involved, and this was England, not America. There were no cover-ups here, no devious lawyers to twist the evidence, just good old-fashioned straightforward trial by media. There had been a 'tragedy' and now there was 'justice'.

When Eileen returned to court for sentencing, the judge gave her fifteen years. The ripple effect was swift and far-reaching. *New Town*'s viewing figures, after taking a slight dip, rose and remained high. Sonia Sutherland had judged the depraved appetites of the viewing public well: the storylines now revolved almost entirely around gangland killings, rapes and incest. Poppy's thyroid, although still giving her a lot of gyp, barely featured. Dr Ditchling's prostate was banished to the outer darkness. Instead we saw previously homespun characters hanging around rainy street corners where neon lights reflected on wet tarmac just like in American films. We peered at murky scenes in lock-ups and car parks. Everything was underlit. Everyone wore black. There was even swearing; Michael Hawker, that previously frustrated scriptwriter we met in more innocent times, was allowed a free hand. *New Town* now resembled *GoodFellas*, and any suggestion that it was set on a naff estate in south-east England had been forgotten. Sonia secured the services of a couple of American has-beens, and the conversion was complete. Children in playgrounds started referring to the show as '*Nu Town*'.

Eileen's legal team were granted the right to appeal, but nobody seemed to hold out much hope. Even Paul thought that this was a formality. His ever-expanding circle of friends were so impressed that he had been close to a celebrity murder that he never had to buy his own dinner. He even started to get a bit of sex on the back of his criminal associations, although it was never more than a melancholy reminder of happier times with Danny. Such were the benefits of Eileen being guilty that Paul ended up believing the verdict himself.

She wrote to him from prison, asking him to visit, and when he showed the letter around the dinner table it was read aloud to a chorus of squawks and gasps. 'Dearest Paul,' she wrote (Paul glowed with pride), 'I am bearing this as best I can but I am so lonely. I can put up with a lot the cold the food the women in here who are a pack of hyennes but I miss my friens and I miss you most of all please come and see me when you can I cant promise much in the way of hospitalaty but you know me I put on a brave face darlin love E xxx.'

He was on a train the next day, rattling up the north-west coast towards the godforsaken hole where Eileen was incarcerated. On the way, he read this edifying report in the *Daily Beacon*, the paper that had been largely responsible for her imprisonment. Their serialisation of Pat the Firestarter O'Connor's gangland memoirs had been expensive but successful; now they were looking for more angles on the still-hot Weathers scandal.

SOAP STAR'S PRISON OUTRAGE ran the headline, before explaining that 'inmates of a women's prison where former *New Town* star is currently beginning a fifteen-year sentence for the murder of her husband Jimmy Livesey and his tragic girlfriend Gemma Leeds have occupied the prison canteen in a sit-down protest at having to share their cells with a MAN. "Eileen Weathers is not a real woman and she should not be in a women's prison," says a spokeswoman for the protesters, forty-eight-year-old murderer Jackie Clubbs. "None of us feel safe with her around. We've seen how she looks at us in the showers." The shadow Home Secretary today agreed that there were possible grounds for DNA testing of prisoners whose biological gender was "in reasonable doubt".'

Paul threw the paper on to the floor. It fell open at a page of chatline ads featuring Stunning TS Beauties.

Eileen looked thinner than usual, and no longer enjoyed the ministrations of Lorraine, her personal make-up artist, but Paul thought she had acquired a kind of beauty that had, perhaps, been lacking before. Instead of looking like an ageing party girl, she now had the dignity of a classical actress, Vanessa Redgrave or Maggie Smith, casually dressed for rehearsal; the role of Clytemnestra, perhaps…Her hair was straight but clean, swept back from her face, revealing an ivory brow. The skin around her eyes bore a tracery of fine lines that spoke of suffering bravely borne. Her voice, usually booming, was soft and modulated.

'Thanks for coming, darlin',' she said, as if frightened of being overheard. 'They were starting to say that all my old friends had deserted me. Oh, well, you certainly do find out who your real friends are when you're in a tight spot.' She squeezed Paul's arm across the table; a vicious-looking prison officer sneered at the gesture.

'How have you been?' asked Paul, not knowing what to say and feeling suddenly ashamed of dining out on Eileen's miscarriage of justice.

'Oh, don't worry about me,' she said. 'I've put up with worse. Compared with my Nana Scammell's, this is a holiday camp.'

'What's the cell like?'

'Bit like a *New Town* dressing room, darlin'. Cramped but homely. There's always someone spying on me, but I'm used to that. It's like the paparazzi, innit?'

'And what do you do with your time?'

'Sleep. Read books. Avoid the bloody awful prison food. And they're getting me a job, darlin'.'

'Oh, that's good. Isn't it? What are you doing?'

'You won't believe this,' said Eileen, staring at a broken fingernail. 'They've put me in the prison laundry.'

Paul thought for a moment that she was going to burst into tears – but instead Eileen ran a hand through her hair and laughed long and loud. The rest of the room fell silent at a sound so familiar from TV. Television-viewing was strictly rationed, but they all made a point of watching *New Town*.

'From one fucking launderette to another, eh? Well, at least I know what I'm doing.'

The guard sneered again. 'Service wash, darlin'?' cackled Eileen, and the rest of the cons laughed with her.

'Has anyone from the show been in touch?'

'Sonia came in. Two-faced bitch. Said how sorry she was, bla bla bla, but she spent the whole time looking around and taking notes and then she had tea with the governor. Can't say I've seen any personal benefits as a result. Charming. Said she was very proud of my Bafta nomination, that she would accept the award for me if I was unable to attend in person, thanked me for my contribution to the success of the show. Contribution? I *am* the show! Just wait until I'm not in it any more. Then they'll see. As for the Baftas – oh, they're really going to give me a night off for that, aren't they? I can just see the limo pulling up at the prison gates now.'

Her voice was getting louder; she checked herself, pressed a hand against her forehead and breathed deeply. 'I try very hard not to be bitter, Paul. Sometimes it's not easy. I'm sorry, I didn't mean to take it out on you.'

'That's what I'm here for,' said Paul, who enjoyed the role of murderer's moll. 'Any news from your lawyers?'

'We're working on it, darlin'. I'm sure they'll come up with something.'

'Of course they will. You're innocent.' The words tasted like gall and wormwood in Paul's mouth.

'I know that. Sometimes I think I'm the only person in the world who does.'

It was a travesty, that trial. The judge should have stopped it, and he should have done the *Beacon* for contempt. It's a disgrace that you're in here at all.'

'Yes. That's what some of the girls are saying.'

'Oh. You heard about that, did you?'

'Course I did. Can't keep anything like that quiet.'

'So they occupied the canteen, then?'

'What? Did they shit. You must stop believing what you read in the papers, darlin'.'

'So who's been complaining?'

'Some slag who got pissed off because I wouldn't bump pussy with her.'

'You mean…'

'Well, they all want to be the first one to fuck the TV star, don't they?'

'My God,' said Paul, who had seen this kind of thing on television. 'So it's true, then.'

'What, dykes in prison? Oh, darlin'!' Eileen rolled her eyes to heaven.

'It must be awful for you.'

'I know how to take care of myself.'

'And what if they decide to put you in a men's prison?'

'They won't.'

'How can you be so sure?'

Eileen looked Paul straight in the eye. 'Because, darlin', they're going to do a DNA test on me and that will squash once and for all these silly fucking stories about me being a sex change.'

'Will it?'

Eileen took a deep breath, as if she was about to call Paul every name under the sun, but then paused and exhaled in a long sigh.

'Yes, darlin', it will.'

'So why is everyone so sure that it won't?'

'Because they know I can't sue.'

'Some people would say,' said Paul, 'that there's no smoke without fire.'

'A rather unfortunate turn of phrase, darlin', considering what I'm in for, but we'll let that pass. So do you really want to know the truth, then? The whole truth and nothing but?'

'That was our agreement.'

'Got your notebook?'

'Of course.'

'Then listen carefully.' Eileen shuffled forward in her seat. The mean guard edged closer. If there were doubts about anyone's biological gender, thought Paul, it certainly wasn't Eileen's.

'I know what they say about me. They say I was born a boy. That I used to be a renter in the West End. Then I started performing in drag in the strip clubs, under the name Kiki de Londres. Stop me if I get any of this wrong, darlin'.'

'No,' said Paul, scribbling, 'that sounds about right.'

'Then in the '60s – or was it the '70s? Nobody seems to be able to agree on that one – I disappeared for a while and came back with a little something missing. And that explains why I can't have children, because I'm not really female. And I've been trying to cover up the truth ever since. Yes? Does that just about cover it?'

'I think so,' said Paul, wondering if he'd just heard a confession.

'Well, it should do, darlin'. I mean, I should know that story better than anyone. And you know why?'

Paul swallowed. 'Why?'

'Because I made it up. I started the rumours. It's all my own work.'

'You said it started as a joke when you couldn't have children with Charlie.'

'Oh, did I?'

'But Charlie had children later, didn't he?'

'Yes. No question about that old goat's fertility.' She shuddered.

'So what's the truth?' asked Paul. 'Would anyone in her right mind claim to be a sex change when she's not?'

'Just trying to keep myself out of trouble, as usual,' laughed Eileen.

'Go on.'

'It all goes back to the early '70s, like everything else in my story. London was full of girls like me, shagging and modelling and getting recording contracts, and there was more than one of them who didn't have the DNA to match, I can tell you, naming no names. We always used to laugh about it. There were plenty of men – famous men now – who weren't averse to a little bit extra down there.'

'But you…why you?'

'I'll tell you, darlin'. I got knocked up. There.'

'Bloody hell.'

'That's what I thought. I'd got this boyfriend, right, who was a very high-profile gangster; we'll call him Pete. He was a wonderful man, darlin', but he couldn't keep it in his pants. And I'm not surprised; it was the biggest one I ever saw, size of that old lezzer's truncheon.' She whispered, and flicked her eyes towards the ever-vigilant guard. 'There, that got you interested. Oh, he was a rogue, my Pete. Screwed everything that moved, including members of our royal family. It was an open secret, darlin'. And we all thought that we would be the one to tame him. So I fell pregnant. Not on purpose; I wasn't that cheap. But after I got over the shock, I thought it might be a way of, you know, keeping him at home. Still he wasn't interested, and so I decided to get rid of it. Well, I was young, I was just starting out, I'd got my big break and I didn't want to be one of those awful actresses with some sad little brat in tow. There would be plenty of time for that, I thought. And so I disappeared, went somewhere sunny and had it done, made a little holiday of it…And since then, nothing. Never been able to conceive. Not a thing. Barren as a stone, darlin'.'

'I'm so sorry.'

'Don't be. I've never met the man whose child I'd want to bear. Lucky escape.'

'So how did all this…?'

'I came home off my little sunshine holiday, and the papers were there to meet me. You see, I'd been on telly a bit by this time, so suddenly everyone was interested in this actress who was knocking around with a gangster. They all wanted to know where I'd been, what I'd been doing. I wasn't going to tell them I'd just had an abortion, was I? Just wasn't done in those days. But I had to tell them something, so I thought I'd give them a story that would satisfy their curiosity but would be too shocking to print. So I said, very airy and matter of fact as I arrived at the airport, "Oh, it's nothing, boys…Just a tiny operation…I feel like a new woman!" And they believed it. The rumours went round and round and got louder and louder, and in the end people actually started to say on very good authority that they'd had me back in the '60s when I was a boy. That I used to work on the meatrack in Piccadilly. That my real name was Arthur, or something equally fucking ridiculous. And all because of some silly little joke I told to cover up my real… pain…'

'But the details. The photographs! Kiki de Londres, who's she?'

'All made up, darlin', every bit of it. This is a one hundred per cent biological female, as the DNA tests, if they ever happen, will prove.'

'Can I believe you?'

Eileen tossed her head back and laughed again. 'What, you want to have a look?' Paul blushed. 'Thought not, although there's no need to turn your nose up, darlin', because plenty have paid good money for a peek at my pussy.' The guard hovered a little closer. 'Not you, darlin'. You can't afford it on your wages.'

Visiting time was over.

Paul cried on the train home to London. He cried for his betrayal of Eileen, her dignity in prison, her grace under pressure. He cried for himself too, deserted by the man he loved and destined to journey through life alone. This was probably the thing he cried about most, and by the time he had got past Crewe he was enjoying a good old weep. Train journeys always made him feel melancholy, a result of having read too many depressing novels, and it had been so many weeks since his last encounter with Danny he was naturally tearful.

He wiped his eyes when he noticed an attractive man staring at him from across the carriage. Paul blew his nose and tried to compose himself to look tragic but available.

And just when everyone was settling down to their new lives, along came the appeal.

Paul hadn't expected much to change and looked forward to a future in which Eileen would gradually fade into a sad but prestigious memory. *New Town* was learning to get along without her very well and had employed a whole new cast, many of them American, who were riding the crest of Sonia Sutherland's success. Everyone was looking forward to the Bafta awards in May, at which *New Town* was up for best continuing drama, and Eileen personally nominated as best actress. Of course, she wouldn't win – but it would give everyone something to get misty-eyed about in the close-up shots. That and the gallons of free booze.

The appeal was announced in a few quiet paragraphs in the papers, merely noting that it was due to take place and that Eileen's legal team had 'no comment' on their client's prospects – well-accepted legal jargon meaning 'the poor cow hasn't got a chance and can rot in prison for all we care'. There wasn't too much gloating, even from the Leeds and Livesey families; in fact, there wasn't very much interest at all.

The judge seemed to be half asleep. There were no reporters in the courtroom apart from one keen young freelancer. Paul went along out of loyalty, and because he'd promised Eileen that he would cover it for the book – which now seemed less likely than ever to see the light of day.

Just as things were droning into a soporific stupor, Paul heard the words that snapped him wide awake.

'I call to the stand Mr Danny Attard.'

The doors opened, and Danny swaggered into court. He was wearing a suit, his hair was a fraction longer than its usual zero crop, and the sight of him nearly made Paul throw up.

Danny confirmed his identity, caught Paul's eye up in the gallery and winked. Paul was his slave again.

'Mr Attard,' asked Eileen's counsel, 'I believe you have new evidence that has a bearing on this case.'

'Yes,' said Danny clearly and confidently.

'I ask the court to admit Exhibit A.'

There was a nod from on high.

'Ladies and gentlemen of the jury,' began the defence in dramatically restrained tones, 'what you are about to see is a video recording that has been sent to the witness.'

The judge looked puzzled.

'It is what is known as webcam footage, your honour.'

The judge was none the wiser, but the lights dimmed and a monitor flickered into life. There was no sound at first, other than a dull hiss, but dialogue would have been drowned out by the screams from the public gallery.

There, on screen, was Gemma Leeds. She was nearly naked and holding a lighted match.

chapter twelve

Gemma was wearing her bra and panties, a sweet little set that Jimmy had bought her by mail order, made of the sheerest red mesh with a black lace trim and love hearts picked out at the hips and nips in white sequins. She was modelling for the camera, which cut off her head and legs.

'Ooh, I love them, Jimmy, I really love them!'

'Yeah,' said Jimmy's voice (off). 'Now let's see how quickly you can get them off.'

'Not yet, lover,' said Gemma, waving the lighted match dangerously close to the cheap, combustible fabric that covered her boobs. 'You know what happens first.'

Jimmy groaned. 'Out of the way, then, bitch,' he said, and bounded in front of the camera. He was not wearing a bra and panties; in fact, he wasn't wearing anything at all. The jury noticed that he was no longer in the tip-top physical condition that had made him a screen heart-throb to millions of spinsters and gay teens.

'Lie down, slave,' said Gemma, capering out of shot. Jimmy parked himself on a black leather Eames chair, leaned back and spread his legs. The more squeamish members of the jury looked away; the other ten, hardened to this sort of thing, carried on viewing.

'You've been a naughty boy,' said Gemma, her voice pitched a little higher than normal, as if she were impersonating a schoolgirl, 'and you're going to be punished.'

'Oh, no, mistress, please.' Jimmy was wide-eyed with fear.

'Yes, you know what happens now.'

'No…please…' Jimmy was sweating, as if in rut.

A burning candle appeared in front of the camera. 'Hope you're all watching this at home, viewers,' said Gemma's voice as she advanced from behind the camera towards Jimmy's prone, flabby body. 'This is going to hurt.'

She straddled him, and Jimmy groaned. There was a massive glitch on the tape, a howl of noise and then the picture returned. Jimmy was writhing and kicking as Gemma straddled him.

'Ow, you bastard, that really fucking hurts!'

Gemma's hand appeared from behind her back, still holding the lighted candle, which had burned down considerably. She must have poured an awful lot of hot wax on to his torso.

'Aaaagh…' Jimmy writhed. Gemma lost her balance, tipped awkwardly to one side and broke her fall with her hand. The candle was lost to view.

'Get off me, you big sow. This is ridiculous.'

Another glitch in the tape, and Gemma disappeared from view.

'Nobody speaks to Mistress Gemma like that,' she said, her voice now rasping. 'You're going to be taught a lesson, pig-boy.'

She reappeared, holding a pair of handcuffs.

'No, stop it, Gem. I don't want the handcuffs.'

She slapped him hard round the face, knocking him back into the chair from which he was attempting to rise.

'Sit back and give me your hands.' There was a click. 'There. Not so cocky now, are you?' Jimmy's wrists were fastened.

'Now you're my slave, you dirty little bastard.'

Gemma carried on unconvincingly in this vein; several of the lawyers thought she was making a very poor show and knew professional dominatrices who did it much better.

There was some half-hearted bouncing around, and then Jimmy's voice, muffled by the black mesh bra, said: ''Ere, hold it, Gem. I can smell burning.'

'Shut up slave. Taste the pain.' She slapped him again.

'Leave it out, you mad bitch. I really can smell…'

Gemma leaped to her feet and screamed. The image was replaced by white lines.

There was silence in the court as the lights went up.

'Mr Attard,' said the defence counsel after a dramatic pause. 'Could you tell us how you came by this footage?'

'It was sent to me.'

'By what means?'

'By e-mail.'

'From whom?'

'A woman called Susan Lloyd.'

'Did the name mean anything to you?'

'Vaguely. She's a *New Town* fan.'

'What sort of fan?'

'One of them real obsessive ones. Runs a couple of websites, and a fan club for Jimmy Livesey. Bit nutty…'

'Have you ever met her?'

'No. I think Jimmy was in contact with her.'

'What makes you think that?'

'Well, he mentioned her occasionally, as a bit of a joke. Said she was stalking him.'

'Do you think she was?'

'Not seriously. She sent him a lot of daft letters, flowers on his birthday, teddies, that sort of thing. There's quite a few like that. Eileen gets it too. Comes with the job.'

'Was there anything more to the relationship between Mr Livesey and Miss Lloyd than simple fan worship?'

'Well,' said Danny, looking down at his huge, shovel-like hands as they rested on the edge of the witness box, 'I think there might have been a bit of…flirting.'

'Flirting?'

'Naughty texts, e-mails, you know. Jimmy was a naughty boy.'

'You mean he slept with his fans?'

'Oh, yeah.'

'Did Mrs Livesey know about this?'

'She turned a blind eye to it.'

'How did Miss Lloyd acquire this footage?'

'They used to have webcam chats.'

'Could you explain to the court what that means, exactly?'

'Sure. You have a little camera attached to your computer, the other person has one at their end, and you can watch what each other is doing.'

'And Mr Livesey and Miss Lloyd…'

'Yeah. I'd walked in on him a couple of times when he was…well, chatting to her.' Danny grinned.

'Exposing himself?'

'Yeah,' said Danny, who formed a fist and waggled it in the air. 'You know.'

'Apparently things had gone a little further than mere masturbation.'

'Seems like it, doesn't it?'

'In fact, Mr Livesey was putting on live sex shows for an audience of one.'

'Yeah. Sue Lloyd said she was too embarrassed to come forward after the accident because it made her look like a pervert.'

'So she watched Mr Livesey and Miss Leeds cavorting together while she…'

'Yeah. And she recorded it and I reckon she was going to sell it.'

'To whom?'

'Other fans. The papers. I don't know. That sort of thing can make a lot of money. Look at that Paris Hilton.'

'But she didn't sell, did she? She kept it to herself.'

'When she found out what happened, she panicked.'

'Why wasn't the footage produced at the original trial?'

'You'll have to ask Miss Lloyd that question,' said Danny. 'I only got hold of it a couple of days ago.'

'And finally, Mr Attard, are you satisfied that this footage is genuine?'

'Genuine?' said Danny, his eyes wide with surprise. 'How could it be fake?

You only have to look at it to see…Well, you know…' He blushed under his tan and looked down at his bitten thumbnails.

'Thank you, Mr Attard, that will be all,' said the defence. 'I would now like to call Miss Susan Lloyd…'

She was a large woman: so large, in fact, that she had trouble mounting the few steps to the witness box. Even when she took the stand, it was a tight squeeze. There were sniggers from the jury.

'Miss Lloyd,' said the judge, after she had corroborated every sentence of Danny's testimony, 'you do realise that withholding evidence is a very serious matter and could lead to a criminal prosecution, do you not?'

She was sweating. 'I know, your lordship. I'm ever so sorry…'

'But under the circumstances,' said the judge, fighting back a smile, 'I think we can overlook your misplaced modesty and concentrate instead on the value of the evidence.'

The prosecution tried hard to demolish Susan Lloyd. He suggested she had fabricated the entire thing, that she was a fantasist who imagined herself in a relationship with Jimmy Livesey, that she was in the pay of Eileen Weathers…He tried so many different attacks, in fact, that in the end the jury was laughing openly at his desperation.

'Well,' they said to one another as they retired to consider their verdict, 'you only have to look at the tape to see what happened. The camera doesn't lie, does it?'

chapter thirteen

Up the red carpet they came, every one-trick pony in the business, all the headline-hungry, talent-free stage-school brats who had managed to inveigle their way on to a TV screen. Limo doors slammed, cameras clicked and whirred, fans whimpered and a gaggle of overexcited journalists ran up and down the line, asking the same lame questions they asked year after year.

'What are you wearing, Jennifer? Is that Valentino?'

'Are you pleased to be back in *Emmerdale*?'

'Is it true that you've had offers from Hollywood?'

'Who do you think will win?'

Those posed photographs, those meaningless quotes, would fill papers and magazines for a fortnight.

The lesser the talent, the longer they spent on the red carpet leading up to the doors of Grosvenor House. The old hands, who were up for best actor or best comedy performance, smiled quickly, waved, stopped for five seconds in front of the photographers, then scuttled inside. The younger stars spent a little longer, posed a little harder, maybe blew kisses. The fading stars, or the hopefuls of whom nobody except a few million magazine readers had heard, worked the carpet so hard they wore holes in it. Some of them nipped back and went around twice.

In the Grosvenor House lobby, millions of pounds' worth of ugly designer clobber was glittering and rustling around the central stairs. Strategic posing points had already been claimed by your more publicity-conscious celebrities, who tried to look casual and relaxed while exposing themselves to as many people as possible. One middle-aged current affairs presenter, who had gained new fame by losing first her husband, then half her body weight, clambered up on to the base of a pillar, where her tiny shred of a gown vied for attention with her scrawny, over-tanned limbs. The older actors sneered at her, the younger ones laughed at her, but everyone talked about her.

There was a bottleneck around the seating plans and much jostling to see who was sitting where. And then, with half an hour to go before dinner was served, they started to descend the curved staircase into the overdecorated hangar of the Great Room. Some hovered at the head of the stairs, waiting until there was a sufficient audience to make an entrance worthwhile. Others hurried ahead in the knowledge that there was a lake of free booze. An army of waiters, each more attractive than the last, plied the thirsty nominees with wine. By the end of the evening, each waiter would have enough phone numbers shoved into his or her pocket to guarantee a lifetime of kiss and tells.

Thick and fast they came at last, glittering down the stairs like a Milky Way of sequins against the rich dark stuff of dinner jackets. To TV viewers the following evening, when the swearing had been edited out, it would look like a Busby Berkeley fantasy of wonderful showbiz nightlife. In fact, it was only four o'clock on a Sunday afternoon.

They kissed and cuddled, they screamed and waved, they put on a convincing show of camaraderie, while inside they envied and hated each other and feared for their own precarious status. The producers, controllers and agents, unrecognised by the public, drew little groups around them like magnets draw iron filings. A journalist, who couldn't get her calls returned before she got a job on a national celebrity magazine, noticed with pride that there was a small queue forming at her table as underdressed nobodies vied for her attention.

Awards ceremonies are the traditional meeting ground for the television business, the only place where colleagues share, for an illusory moment, the sense of togetherness in a wonderful profession. Deals are struck, friendships made and rekindled, projects hatched and romances born. But tonight the tone was different: sharper, tenser, more expectant. Behind the small talk, behind the false smiles, there was only one thing on people's minds.

Eileen Weathers.

Every time a middle-aged blonde swept down the stairs, heads swivelled.

Every time an uncultured female voice broke forth in raucous laughter, ears pricked.

When Sonia Sutherland made her entrance in a Yamamoto creation of ultra-chic severity, the Great Room was hushed – for Sonia, if anyone, would know the answer to the question that hung unspoken on every lip.

Would Eileen get out of prison in time for the best actress award?

But Sonia arrived alone and moved down the staircase with a smile and a nod and nothing more. The throng parted as she reached the floor, and she moved straight in on Damian Davies, the still dazzlingly attractive former star of *New Town*. Rumour had it that Damian was 'slated' to return to the show at an estimated cost of £1 million, and as this kind of rumour did nothing but good Sonia hustled him over to her table and spent a highly visible ten-minute tête-à-tête with the chiselled twenty-four-year-old. Sonia was a quick worker; Damian soon understood that if he really wanted that million-pound gig, he wouldn't be leaving Grosvenor House until the morning. Sonia, a great one for forward planning, had booked a suite.

The lights were dimmed, and a couple of novelty dancers came on in garish orange outfits and twizzled around for ten minutes. This allowed everyone to take their seats and thank God that they had not yet been reduced to providing entertainment at these functions. Then the master of ceremonies appeared and began the ritual of insults and in-jokes that passes for wit at industry awards. The ruder he got, the better his chances, he believed, of a return engagement. When he called the DG of the BBC 'a clapped-out old cunt', his agent called for champagne.

Dinner was served, which was a waste of time and resources, as nobody in the room actually ate anything. Instead they worked their way through life-threatening amounts of wine, determined to be seeing double by the time the awards began.

And begin they finally did. The sports presenters, the news anchors, the single dramas, the factual series, all were duly honoured and instantly forgotten. The winners said a few unwelcome words before being snatched by a smiling hostess who steered them off to the well-hidden backstage areas where journalists were penned like hungry beasts, baying for a few scraps of celebrity waffle.

There was a flurry of interest over best drama series, which was won by a police show (originally 'created' by Sonia Sutherland) which had, said the citation, 'pushed back the boundaries of TV drama'. This meant that an awful lot of women and children had been murdered while some well-dressed attractive people wandered around police stations frowning a lot. Sonia was as pleased as punch with that; her portfolio was doing very nicely.

The next climax came with the nominations for best continuing drama. *New Town* was nominated for the first time since the category had been initiated, which was an achievement in itself, for during the doldrum days of Tracey Reynolds, when the drama revolved around environmental issues and the occasional outbreak of ringworm, the show had been resolutely overlooked. Now that Sonia Sutherland had filled Eastgate with attractive rapists, drug-dealing asylum-seekers, homicidal black men and American gangsters, it could be taken seriously once again as family entertainment.

There was stiff competition from the other channels, of course. The BBC's big continuing drama was also full of criminals and deviants. The commercial stations were bristling with contenders, some of them set in hospitals, some in police stations, some in farming communities or in the ex-industrial north, but all of them sharing community values of rape, arson and child abuse.

'…for its originality, its hard-hitting treatment of contemporary social issues, its fearless championing of causes,' ran the all-purpose citation, 'its unflinching portrayal of violence in a changing world…' Sonia was almost screaming; *her* violence, *her* sexual abuse, *her* two-dimensional stereotyping were better than anyone else's, she knew. She poured a drink, longed for a fag and composed her face into a serviceable smile, win or lose.

'And the winner,' said the presenter, fumbling with the envelope, 'is *New Town*.'

Sonia accepted kisses from left and right as her cast bounced up on to the stage to receive the award. She felt – what? Vindicated? Not really, as she never doubted for one moment that she would win. Triumphant? Yes, but only when she looked towards the grinning man-child face of Damian Davies, her plaything for the night.

Little did she know that her days at *New Town* were numbered, that this time next year she'd be calling in favours to scrounge an invitation to the awards ceremony where now she reigned as queen.

Benjamin Oluwatobi was up on stage, rabbiting on about the show. '…proof that there is a place for serious social issues in a mainstream popular drama…' The microphone was grabbed by Leah Wilkinson, now the unchallenged bitch-queen of the Bromley lot. 'This one's for Gemma!' she screamed drunkenly. It was what the audience wanted to hear, and they rose to their feet, hoping they looked sincere on camera. Some of them squeezed out a tear for a colleague cut down in her prime. It mattered little that Gemma's reputation was forever soiled by the sordid webcam footage so recently revealed in court, and soon to be selling for good money on every dodgy market stall in the country.

The applause died down, people returned to their seats and showed a polite interest in the next – the penultimate – category, best actor. The men's awards were usually the climax, but this year, in acknowledgement of the extraordinary circumstances, it was ladies last.

A rotund middle-aged man waddled up to receive an award, his tenth, for a drama in which he'd enjoyed an implausible romance with an actress less than half his age. There was a ripple of applause, barely audible above the hubbub of speculating voices. Better, more convincing clapping would have to be overdubbed in time for transmission.

An unobtrusive black BMW glided through the streets of west London, past Hammersmith, along the Talgarth Road, through Earl's Court and Knightsbridge, around Hyde Park Corner… The sky was already dark as the car snaked its way up Park Lane, unnoticed, unmarked by the few dogged fans still lurking outside Grosvenor House. A faint smell of hairspray and Chanel No. 5 wafted from the air-conditioning system, the only indication that there was a star in transit…

*

'And the nominations are…' The winner of a TV talent show was awestruck to be reading out a Bafta.

There was a hold-up in Park Lane; a bus and a taxi had tangled and were skewed across the road, blocking traffic. The BMW's window glided down and a female voice, accustomed to command, shouted: 'Move your fucking arses, there's a lady in a hurry here…'

'Barbara Windsor…'

The taxi reversed, its smashed radiator steaming, and wedged its back wheels against the crash barriers.

'Kate O'Mara…'

The driver of the BMW executed a perfect U-turn and, lights flashing and horn blaring, drove against the oncoming traffic back to the nearest cross-lane. As outraged drivers cursed and hooted, a perfectly manicured hand, the nail varnish still wet, emerged from the window and flicked a V-sign.

'Julie Goodyear…'

The BMW careered across three lanes of southbound traffic, mounted the kerb and drove up the pavement, scattering tourists like skittles. Swerving to avoid a pram, it scraped against a lamppost, causing hundreds of pounds' worth of damage to the paintwork. It was still a hundred yards from Grosvenor House.

'…and Eileen Weathers.'
 In the Great Room, you could have heard a pin drop.

The car screeched to a halt in the forecourt, as security guards ran in panic to the doors, fearing a terrorist attack. A thin, pale young man in evening dress got out of the passenger door and, holding it open, offered his hand to a figure within. From the darkness of the car, there was a shimmer of silver.

'And the winner is…'

First the shoes emerged: silver high-heeled slippers, then the legs, gleaming in sheer hosiery, and the skirt, an understated essay in silver and white.

The lights in the Great Room seemed too bright, the air too thick to breathe…

Eileen stood quietly for a moment, breathing deeply, her eyes shut, her hands raised above her head (no unsightly veins for her). And then she smiled, took the pale young man's arm and said: 'Come on, darlin'. I hope we're not late.'

'Oh, my God,' screamed the announcer, 'the winner is Eileen Weathers!'
    The entire profession rose to its feet and cheered, hoping that by so doing they would show solidarity with a sister in difficulties.
    The comedy MC took to the microphone.
    'Of course, as we all know, Eileen's unavoidably detained at one of Her Majesty's holiday camps…well, it makes a change from the Priory. I just hope to God they don't let her play with matches…'
    Eileen stood at the top of the great curved staircase. She had no microphone, no PA. It did not matter. She had grown up on the streets of south London and could make herself heard.
    'Hold your fucking horses, darlin'.'
    Every head turned. Somewhere in the upper gloom, silver stars twinkled as they began their descent.
    The lighting man turned the follow-spot on to the stairs.
    She came down with one hand resting lightly on the banister, head up, heels in, like a Soho showgirl.
    Before she was halfway down, the entire room was cheering, stamping,

whistling, clapping. Paul, who remained on the landing, watched Eileen as she was handed from one handsome man to another and finally, incredibly, lifted on the shoulders of actors to be deposited, as light as a feather, on the stage.

Even the MC was lost for words.

Eileen smiled sweetly, curtsied and, with one gesture of her hand, commanded silence.

"'Ello, darlin's,' she said. 'Mummy's home.'

Monday's newspapers were full of one thing: the dramatic story of Eileen Weathers's release from prison, her 'mercy dash' from a police station in west London, where she'd been taken in an armoured prison van, to Park Lane, in her own chauffeur-driven limo. The miracle of her transformation en route, from dowdy jailbird to thousand-watt superstar. She had achieved more in the back of a van and a BMW than most women or even drag queens could do with a fully equipped dressing room. And then, of course, the entrance into Grosvenor House, the ascent to the stage, the way she had grabbed the award with both hands and raised it above her head like a weapon…

Nobody else got a look-in. *New Town*'s triumph as best continuing drama was an ironic footnote to the main event. The half-starved current affairs presenter who believed that it had all been worthwhile – the divorce, the heartbreak, the hunger and foul breath – just to get her picture on the front pages was disappointed. Nobody was anybody now that Eileen Weathers was back in town.

Not content with occupying pages one through five with her news story, Eileen also commandeered most of the centre pages of the *Daily Beacon*, the paper to which, after much negotiation, she had sold her prison story. This had been delivered to the subeditors before she'd even been released, fresh from the desk of Paul Mackrell.

Before the *Beacon*'s first edition had even hit the news-stands, syndication rights to the feature and its four follow-ups had been sold around the world. It appeared on breakfast tables wherever *New Town* had a following, from Toronto to Turkmenistan.

'In the last few weeks,' began the rousing final passage, 'I've been to hell and back.' Paul left no stop unpulled.

I've lived in a cell with three other women, all of them habitual drug users, two of them lesbians, the other a schizophrenic who screamed all night, every night. I've surrendered the last shreds of privacy to the invading fingers of so-called prison security officers who believed – they said – that I was hiding drugs in my most intimate crevices. I've learned just how low we can sink when we let go of our basic belief in human dignity.

But there are two things I have never let go, no matter how tough things got: my knowledge that I am completely innocent, and my faith that I would one day see justice.

In my darkest hours – and, yes, there were moments when even my hope wavered – I thought this was the price I must pay for what I have always said was a charmed life. After years of basking in public adulation, what could I expect now but the curses and contempt of my cellmates? Oh, they knew how to hurt me. They knew every mistake I'd made, every failed romance, every detail of a life I once thought was private. I tried to put on a brave face – and it was never the physical violence, painful though it was, particularly in the showers, that made me cry. No: it was the verbal abuse, day in, day out. I didn't sleep for nearly six weeks.

Nothing I can say will bring back Jimmy or Gemma. Nothing I can say will ever convince a mind full of hate that I did not want them dead. Before I went into prison, it worried me that people would always believe I was guilty. Now I have come through the fire, and I no longer care. Even if everyone else condemns me, God knows that I am innocent. I stand before Him alone – the only judge I care about. Maybe I will never forgive what has been done to me, maybe I will never regain what has been taken from me – but one thing is for sure. When I am on my deathbed, I will look back on a life that is richer and, yes, fuller than the lives of the millions who accused me. I will bear no grudges, no bitterness. And I will look up to heaven and I will say 'Thank you – for everything.'

chapter fourteen

'...and if that two-faced cunt thinks she can worm her way back into my good books just by taking me out for lunch and dangling her fucking chequebook under my nose, she's got another think coming,' said Eileen, sitting behind the desk at the rebuilt Essex mansion. 'She's got a bloody nerve after all she put me through, the bitch. Well, I'll see her burn in hell before I work for her again.'

Paul crossed Sonia Sutherland's name off a list.

'There have been calls from a number of agents who want to represent you.'

Eileen laughed long and loud, lit a fresh cigarette from the stub of the last and polished off her fifth espresso of the morning.

'Let 'em call! Tell them I'm considering their kind offers. Let them eat their black little hearts out,' she said, removing a fleck of tobacco from her tongue. In prison she'd learned to prefer roll-ups.

'We've got cromalins of the book jacket.'

'Ah, yes, let me see. Hmm...' Eileen picked up a chinagraph pencil and started scribbling. 'No, don't like it. Fucking tacky. Who do they think I am, Joan Bleedin' Collins? No, horrible, too old-fashioned. Ah, that's better. Yes. OK, tell 'em they can go with that one, but for Christ's sake get that wanker Snowdon to do something about the crow's feet. You do the blurb as well. I don't want their semi-literate crap on the cover.'

'And there's a cheque for the final instalment of the advance.'

'Oh, goody, darlin'. Hand it over.'

Paul relinquished £200,000. 'Pay Eileen Weathers,' she said. 'My three favourite words. Now don't you worry, Paul. I'll share nicely. You won't go short.'

'And there's a contract from ITV for the dramatisation.'

'Good.'

'Better make sure you get a good writer on that, Eileen…'

'You, you mean, darlin'? You ever written a script before?'

'I told you, I've done several treatments…'

'Yeah. Need someone experienced for this, darlin'. Already been approached by whats-his-name. What else?'

'The record producer called.'

'Oh, good. Is he still keen?'

'He says he's chosen the songs and already recorded the backing tracks. Just needs your vocals.'

Paul handed Eileen a list.

'Let's see…Hmm, I like it. "Burning Love". "Fire". "Smoke Gets in Your Eyes". "Jailhouse Rock". "Prisoner" – oh, I love Streisand, don't you, Paul?'

'Hmm…'

'And what are we calling this little masterpiece?'

'He wants to call it "Phoenix".'

'As in Pat?'

'As in the mythological fire bird that is reborn out of its own ashes. Personally, I think it's in rather poor…'

'Phoenix,' said Eileen with a smile. 'I like it. Next?'

Since sacking her agent in a fit of pique, Eileen had been using Paul as her PA, her secretary, her companion and auxiliary host at a string of functions. For the first time since Jimmy's ill-fated birthday party, the Essex mansion rang again with laughter and music – the laughter a little harder, the music a little louder than before. Invitations to these soirées were the most sought after in show business – and Eileen issued or withheld them as reward or punishment. Indeed, punishment seemed to be the name of the game. That, and making as much money as was humanly possible.

And the possibilities seemed endless. The British public loves nothing so much as a return from the brink, even when they've pushed the poor bastard over it themselves, and Eileen was welcomed back into the nation's affections never again to leave. She had been, as the title of her new autobiography had it, *To Hell and Back*. She had loved and lost and all that stuff. And thanks to some clever PhotoShop work, not to mention an arsenal of 'crèmes' and 'serums' that plumped out her wrinkles, she was looking pretty good for a woman of fifty-five who has spent a few months in prison. Now she was out, she thanked God and the authorities for the dreadfulness of prison food. She'd lost over a stone – and being slim is the ultimate proof of human worth.

Of course, *New Town* wanted her back. They wanted her back so badly that Nick Needs came to her house day after day with ever-more-inflated offers and assurances. She could work three days a week for the same salary as before. For more than before. Two days, for still more. With no restrictions in her contract about other work. But somehow Eileen just couldn't make up her mind.

While she was prevaricating, wondering how far Channel Six would go to get her back, she did a few high-profile chat show appearances, allowed a camera crew into the Essex mansion to do a highly organised reality show and signed a contract for *An Audience with Eileen Weathers*. She did a couple of ads, a couple of voice-overs and in less than a month earned about £500,000. 'Chicken feed,' she snarled at Paul, who would have been happy with just one per cent of that money in payment for his services. 'Don't worry, darlin',' said Eileen, if ever he looked morose, 'our ship is coming in.'

When Nick Needs finally offered Eileen a deal so stupidly generous that even she blushed, she decided that Six had suffered enough, and she'd give them a couple more years of her working life before retiring to a sun-drenched private island somewhere in the Caribbean. Sonia Sutherland had concocted an insane storyline for her return: Maggie would be revealed as 'the Godmother' behind a series of brutal gangland slayings, and would swan back into Eastgate in a designer wardrobe with a string of competing young love interests.

And then Sonia was sacked. Not because *New Town* was doing badly; since Eileen's departure, the figures remained high enough to keep the shareholders quiet. Not even because of the outlandish nature of her storylines – the critics lapped them up and praised her 'realism', particularly in an episode in which Bernard Johnson was shot at point-blank range in a barber shop by a competing black gangster who 'iced him' in a 'turf war'.

No, she was sacked by Channel Six because of that little list she wrote long, long ago when she first got the job, which, you will remember, had been covertly photocopied by a 'cleaner'. The cleaner was a stringer for Gavin Graham, of course.

Gavin had sat on the list, saving it for a rainy day.

The rainy day came when Eileen got out of prison, won the Bafta, refused to resume their former relationship (professional or personal) and even had the nerve not to return his calls. Gavin, his publicist's pride piqued by this unusual display of independence, struck Eileen where he thought it would hurt most, by attacking *New Town*. He sold the list to the *Herald*, who worked up the required fury about bringing Channel Six into disrepute. They pointed out that Sonia had used the words 'wanker', 'nigger' and 'poof'. They hinted at lesbianism in her admiration of Tricia Marvell's tits. They made much of her contempt for senior audiences ('Older viewers? No, fuck 'em'). No amount of retractions from Sonia Sutherland could undo the damage. Bernard Johnson refused to support her claim that she was using 'the N word' in its modern, reclaimed sense. 'In fact,' he said, 'I believe Sutherland's treatment of black characters is inherently racist.'

And so Sonia Sutherland followed Tracey Reynolds and a dozen other disgraced *New Town* producers into the ex-files. When Gemma Leeds's family read about her curt dismissal of their dead daughter ('Job done') they started ululating all over again, and filed a hefty suit for mental anguish.

Sonia survived. She went on to develop a police show for an 'edgy, youth-orientated' cable channel. It was about a sexy young detective sergeant battling to make the force a better place for black and gay officers to work in. It was called *PC-PC*, and Damian Davies was 'attached'.

New Town did not fare so well. Sonia's dismissal, far from getting the brand out of the mire, simply convinced viewers, critics and Channel Six shareholders that it was past its sell-by date. One dark day in June, just weeks before *New Town* would have celebrated its thirtieth anniversary, Nick Needs announced to a hushed press conference that the final episode would be aired at the end of August, making way for 'an exciting raft of new prime-time dramas for Six'.

The never-ending story was over.

Unlike the rest of the cast, Eileen wasn't unemployed for long. As the gates of the Bromley lot were clanging shut for the last time, she was starting her first day's shooting on a brand-new drama for the BBC entitled *JailBirds*, set (where else?) in a women's prison and featuring just enough lesbian overtones (not to mention generous shots of tit and muff) to grab and maintain an enormous audience. Eileen had secured a regular cameo role for Terri Lee as a kindly prison chaplain; the rest of her former *New Town* colleagues could go hang.

Another little bit of casting news made the front pages. Damian Davies, who for weeks had been 'hotly tipped' for the lead role of Sonia Sutherland's new drama *PC-PC*, was announced as the latest recruit to *JailBirds*, playing Eileen's son. What the papers didn't know is that he expressed his gratitude to his new co-star in the only way he knew how. Sonia was utterly, comprehensively abandoned.

JailBirds was a hit – an instant, massive hit that almost made audiences forget that they had ever seen the stars in any other roles before. *New Town* was being written out of the history books as an embarrassment. Property developers bought up the Bromley lot and planned to convert it into a real-life new town that would soon become a byword for anti-social behaviour far worse than anything depicted on screen. Pantomimes that year were greatly enriched by the *New Town* diaspora. Steve Seddon returned to porn, which is what he was really cut out for, and within a year had moved to California. Tyrone D launched a brief pop career and then went the way of all fading stars, trading on his 'celebrity' status in a series of shows set on farms, in jungles and, inevitably, in rehab.

Marjorie Mayhew retired and bred pugs.

Leah Wilkinson married well and gave up the profession.

Tim Boreham, who had never known adult life outside the show, had a massive breakdown and was confined to a private sanatorium.

And what of Paul? In the months following Eileen's release, he had managed, among other things, to finish off 'their' book. *To Hell and Back* was published on a massive wave of publicity, serial rights were sold all over the world, and Eileen signed over 2.5 per cent of the royalties to her collaborator. When she got the job in *JailBirds*, she was obliged to pull out of a book tour, leaving Paul to face disgruntled readers in chilly bookshops across the country. As word of her defection got around, shoppers stayed away in their droves, and Paul spent many lonely hours sitting at tables, hidden by a piles of *To Hell and Back*, failing to sell or sign any copies. Things came to a head one rain-sodden afternoon in Chester, when he was approached by a confused-looking woman in a department store who asked him: 'Do you sell tights?'

He packed up his pens and went home.

But where was 'home' now? The Waterloo flat seemed cold and lonely after Paul's adventures of the last year. He couldn't write; every time he picked up his notebook, the pages curled and torn after multiple scribblings and crossings-out, he felt a wave of nausea. He took to drink, and when that did nothing but give him a headache, he took to the gym, where at least he sometimes made a friend in the sauna. He missed Danny, he missed Eileen – who no longer needed him as a secretary-cum-companion – and he felt all the agonies of withdrawal. For he on honeydew hath fed, he muttered, remembering the sweetness of Danny's kisses, and drunk the milk of paradise.

And then, of course, the phone rang. Guess who?

'Darlin',' she said, as if it was only half an hour since her last call, 'you never call, you never write, your old mum is beginning to wonder if you don't love her any more.'

'Hello, Eileen. How's it going?'

'Fantastic, darlin'!' she boomed down the line. 'I'm a fucking superstar, but you don't need me to tell you that.'

'What can I do for you?' Paul felt curiously aggrieved, as if he were a plaything that Eileen picked up or tossed aside according to her childish whim.

'You can take the ice cubes out of your arsehole for starters, lover. Come over for lunch on Sunday. Day off, no press, no charity stuff, just the family at home. And that means you.'

'Thanks, I'd love to.'

'And if you're not busy tonight…'

'Yes?' He was, in theory, but he was prepared to cancel.

'Well, I've got some bloody awards do to go to, and I haven't got a date, being a single career girl these days, and I wondered if you wouldn't mind being seen on the arm of a wrinkled old hag in a designer frock just one more time.'

'I thought you and…'

'Please say you will, darlin'. It's not a bad one, it's the…What's it called?' She shouted to someone else in the room. 'Oh, yes, the Brits. Lots of pop stars overdosing in the green room. Can you stand it? We've got a nice table. Come on. I'll buy you a new suit.'

Paul had always dreamed of going to the Brits, ever since he was a clandestine *Smash Hits* reader. And there was a rather nice little Armani number he'd seen during an idle hour in Selfridges…

'That's my boy,' said Eileen, reading his mind. 'Car will pick you up at six. Oh, aren't I a lucky girl to have such a handsome date? Makes me feel young again!'

Paul wasn't fooled for a second, as he knew perfectly well that he was at best a 'walker', a 'beard' for Eileen's burgeoning relationship with Damian Davies. Their affair was the talk of the messageboards, but, considering the age gap, not to mention the fate of the previous 'Mr Weathers', they judged it too early to go public. There was also the minor inconvenience of Damian's wife, a pretty blonde Liverpudlian former soap star who was already consulting Gavin Graham about how best to handle her 'love split' when the time came.

Paul e-mailed all his friends, telling them to look out for him on telly, and jumped on a bus to Oxford Street.

That night at the Brits was the first of many in the public eye, not to mention 'family' dinners in the gorgeously restored Essex mansion. There was little doubt that Eileen and Paul enjoyed each other's company – and given that so many of her older friends were either dead or banished to Coventry, Paul now counted as a long-standing confidant. Terri Lee was often at the mansion, pawing some young protégé (he was working his way through the sparks, grips and camera crew of *JailBirds*); Damian Davies put in the occasional appearance. Of Danny there was no sign; he was 'working abroad', according to Eileen, but she wasn't sure as what.

Soon, Eileen and Paul were a recognised couple-about-town. He was referred to as her 'constant companion' in your more discreet society pages. The celebrity mags likened him to David Gest and wondered if there was another Weathers wedding on the way.

Paul was laughing about this one night as they made their way back to the Essex mansion after a terrible movie premiere, the car purring along the A11, the sickly orange glow of streetlamps adding their own nightmare rhythm of light and dark, light and dark.

'They're very keen to marry us off, aren't they?' he said, rather drunk. 'Honestly, this celebrity culture we live in is bloody ridiculous.'

'Is it, darlin'?' said Eileen, staring out of the window at the gruesome bungalows that lined the road.

'I mean, if they can't get a story they just make it up. You and me! God, that's just so stupid.'

Eileen sighed and turned up her collar. 'Really, darlin'? I suppose it is.'

There was something in her voice that Paul didn't quite like.

'Well…I mean, what a hoot…'

'Yes, Paul, I think you've made your point.'

There was silence as they sped away from town. Paul had a sudden, sobering fear that Eileen was hoping to be seduced. He wanted to say something to break the spell – anything would do – but his tongue cleaved to the roof of his mouth.

As they left the sodium glow of London behind them, heading into the blind darkness of Essex, Eileen spoke.

'You know, darlin', when you get to my age you realise there's more to life than cock.'

'I didn't mean…'

'There's such a thing as companionship. Friendship. Trust. Support.'

'Of course, and I really…'

'But if you think it's so ridiculous, so stupid…' She was mimicking his voice: posh, and slightly poofy.

'I didn't mean that. I'm sorry if I…'

'It's all right, darlin'. Keep your hair on. I know when I'm not wanted.'

'Oh, Eileen, for heaven's sake.'

The car was approaching the mansion; Paul could see the old-fashioned carriage lights that marked the entrance to the drive winking ahead. They were home.

'How about it, then?' said Eileen, resting a manicured hand on the leg of Paul's expensive new suit.

'Er…what?'

'God, you don't expect me to go down on one knee, not in this dress.'

'I…'

The car crunched to a halt on the gravel drive. 'Paul,' said Eileen, looking him full in the face, 'will you marry me?'

chapter fifteen

And so Paul Mackrell, the nervous, pasty-faced scribbler from the backstreets of Waterloo, found himself on the cover of *Hello!* magazine, *OK* magazine, *Closer* magazine, *Now* magazine, *Heat* magazine and *Saga* magazine, pilloried more or less openly as the fourth but possibly not final Mr Eileen Weathers. The ceremony was an intimate affair in a National Trust property with a couple of dozen friends and family and a team of photographers. Paul's parents and sister were hideously embarrassed by the whole business as they had hoped that Paul would one day settle down with another nice intellectual young man and lead a quiet, respectable life. Eileen's parents were of course dead, and her brother Keith and sister Rose were unavailable or NBWI. Everyone had too much to drink apart from Eileen, who sped off after the reception to join Damian Davies at a discreet hotel in Holland Park, where she celebrated her wedding night in style. Paul spent the night in the Essex mansion with a young Brazilian caterer.

Married life soon settled into a routine. Paul kept his flat at Waterloo ('independence is important for men,' Eileen told him) but was free to come and go at the Essex mansion; indeed, he often had chores to do there, workmen to oversee, photographers to admit. The newlyweds kept up their attendance at openings and parties for a while, at least until Gavin Graham (back in favour) felt that they were sufficiently established in the public eye. Eileen worked hard all day, every day on *JailBirds*, and during her rare moments of leisure she gave tirelessly to charity and to Damian Davies. His little blonde wife had developed an addiction to prescription painkillers, which was handy.

Paul was working too: at least that was the official line. He was within spitting distance of finishing his new novel, which was mostly about a young writer's life-changing affair with a half-Maltese gangster, and was actually getting some interest from publishers on the strength of his being Eileen Weathers's husband. Unfortunately, when those publishers realised that this was 'a gay novel', they were quick to pass. He was also working on a handful of screenplays, which Eileen assured him (as part of an unofficial pre-nuptial agreement) were 'a shoo-in', given her clout with the commissioning editors. And yet, despite warm interest in *Our Lady of the Flowers* and *Prancing Nigger* from all quarters, nobody would ever go beyond 'a cautious amber'. He picked up a bit of development money here and there, he even got as far as submitting a treatment for the Genet project to Channel Six. 'The crime and gangster elements are gripping as far as they go,' came back the reply, 'but in terms of audience engagement we need someone more mainstream than a drug-addicted drag queen in the lead role. Could you redevelop it as a role for Tim Boreham?' Paul thought that, on the whole, he couldn't, and put *Our Lady of the Flowers* on a back burner.

Meanwhile, things were moving fast on the screen adaptation of *To Hell and Back*, but Paul's contribution had been limited to answering calls and taking messages. This remained a bone of contention between Mr and Mrs Mackrell; he thought he should have been in sole charge of the dramaturgy, while she preferred to hand it over to an extremely experienced and highly paid TV writer with a string of hit series to his credit. 'You're too close to the subject matter, darlin',' she would say, when Paul appeared at breakfast with a face like a smacked arse. 'And come on, it's hardly your thing, is it? Not nearly intellectual enough for you.'

After a year of marriage, Paul added up his earnings – the income that he had honestly gained through his own effort – and found that it amounted to less than he had earned as an adult education teacher. One bad morning, he called the school and asked if he could have his job back. The departmental secretary laughed openly and said it would be great to see him for a drink sometime.

Out in Essex, Paul had little to do but vegetate in comfort. In London, he had his friends…but all they wanted to talk about was Eileen, and half of them would have sold their stories for a very reasonable price if asked. Strange men lurked outside Paul's Waterloo bachelor pad, and not the type of strange men he would have liked. These were professional doorsteppers, just waiting to see him bring someone unsuitable home so that they would have their MR EILEEN'S GAY LOVE NEST story. On one drunken, ill-advised trip to a nearby sauna, he even saw one of the same strange men staking out the steam room. He wasn't sure if the poor soul was there on duty or just trying to warm up after sitting in a freezing car all day.

Married life was not all it's cracked up to be. Paul was lonely, he was bored – and there was nothing he could do to relieve it. He spent hours, whole days sometimes, in online chatrooms. It was as bad as being a self-employed writer – but at least then he had his freedom. Now he was just a bird in a gilded cage.

Not even that: he couldn't sing. Every time a journalist approached Paul for an interview, he or she was told by Gavin Graham that Paul was 'strictly off-limits'. Eileen went out of her way to impress on her husband that she was protecting him from the tabloid press. It was almost as if, for whatever reason, she didn't want Paul to talk to anyone. When she went away for a long weekend to Paris with Damian Davies, she left Paul a note on the breakfast bar. 'Have a wonderful time, darlin'. Remember: careless talk costs lives! E xxx'.

Bored out of his mind, he spent Saturday morning browsing through the catalogue of an online escort agency, and eventually plumped for the one who looked most like Danny, although without his brutish charms. When he arrived, he barged straight past Paul and said 'So this is where she lives, then? Wow?' before giving himself an unguided tour of the Essex mansion.

Five hours later, pseudo-Danny left with £500 in his pocket and a SIM card stuffed with photographs which he felt might come in useful.

Paul drank himself to sleep with Chivas Regal. When he awoke, feeling utterly rank, the Filipina housemaid rolled him a joint, and from that point on became his regular dope dealer. Days passed in a blur of rented cock, Eileen's booze and Acolola's spliffs. When Paul saw Eileen, he tended to shuffle past her, clutching his head, on the way to the bathroom. He found it hard to bear the full wattage of her personality, especially as she was on a professional and personal high. She looked younger than ever – and, despite the predictable rumours, this was not the result of any kind of surgical 'freshen-up' but simply due to a fabulous sex life with a man less than half her age. 'You should try it, babe,' she said to Paul, who had not yet told her that he was lavishing masses of 'their' money on paid companions.

As is right and fitting in a celebrity memoir, Paul's life was on a rapid downward spiral, and he would have ended up in rehab or worse had he not received a wake-up call. No, this was not a sudden blinding message from God. Nor was it the result of reading *The Road Less Travelled*. It wasn't even a sudden conversion to Kabbalah; he may have been a rich woman's underemployed husband, but it hadn't got that bad.

No. Destiny came knocking in a much more dangerous form.

Danny.

It was the end of a bad week. The weather was horrible, one of those late winter days when it seems that spring will never come, the sun will never shine again, it will never be warm. Paul spent hours in bed, furiously typing on Eileen's discarded PowerBook, talking to his imaginary friends and occasionally scribbling thousand-word rants that even he admitted would never turn into novels. He relieved his frustration by drinking and smoking and masturbating; he was so depressed by now that he couldn't even get it up with rent boys any more. That didn't stop him hiring them, and doing things to them, but it was strictly one-way traffic. At the age of thirty-six, Paul was to all intents and purposes impotent.

Thanks to Eileen's credit at the local Threshers, and to Acolola's endless supply of high-grade skunk, Paul needed never be sober. After several months of this Chivas-and-spliff diet, he had gained weight around his waist and tits, but his face was haggard. He was nervous, unable to sleep properly, but prone to pass into an unconsciousness that seemed much like death. Sometimes he got confused about what day it was, and had to ask Acolola. She was always cheerful, made him sandwiches which he rarely ate, rolled his joints and kept his bed linen clean. At least the Essex mansion was a comfortable prison. Before long, Paul had become a complete agoraphobic. He never went to his Waterloo flat any more. Burglars broke in, found nothing worth taking but took it anyway – and that included a box of floppy disks on which Paul had stored all the working materials for his second novel. They were dumped in the river.

Friday came around – Paul knew it was Friday, because *JailBirds* had been on the night before – and he awoke, for some reason, feeling almost well. True, he had polished off the usual amount of Chivas the night before, watching the images of Eileen and Damian swimming before his eyes on the giant TV screen. True, he had puffed his way through several grammes of Acolola's finest, and left her tuna sandwiches untouched. But for some reason his head was clear.

He got up, took a shower, shaved and dressed himself in clean clothes. Today, he thought, he would go into London. He would see an old friend for lunch. He would call a few editors, rustle up some work, make a fresh start. He looked back at his life over the last year – what little he could remember of it – with disgust. This was not Paul Mackrell, the popular, witty dinner guest, author of the promising debut novel *The Frozen Heart*! This was some downtrodden victim, a chewed-up, spat-out by-product of the industrial process called celebrity.

Enough was enough. He'd been blinded by it all – by Eileen's fame and wealth, by Danny's undeniable charms, by the money and the notoriety and the gossip – but now his eyes were open. It was all worthless. Eileen couldn't act, couldn't write, could do nothing except get headlines. As for Danny – well, Danny was a long time ago. One thing Paul had learned from frequenting whores in the last few months was that they all had their act – up until the money was handed over, at least – and every act was much like Danny's. 'He was nothing but a cheap prostitute,' said Paul out loud, and felt much better for it.

He was descending the brand-new staircase, a bright clattery arrangement of steel girders, when he heard a key in the lock of the front door. It couldn't be Acolola – she was working down in the kitchen already. Eileen wasn't expected back until the following week. Paul stopped in his tracks.

The door opened, and a tanned hand appeared around the frame.

It was Danny.

Paul's heart fluttered. He hesitated on the step, uncertain whether to stand there and denounce him or to run into his arms.

Danny stepped into the hall, closed the door quietly behind him and locked it. He was not smiling.

'Danny,' said Paul. 'Long time no see.' He tried to sound nonchalant, but his voice was wavering.

Danny said nothing. He glared at Paul from beneath those famous beetling brows and slunk off towards the living room.

'Danny! Wait!' Paul found himself running after him. He checked himself, slowed to a less degrading pace and sauntered (he hoped) to join him.

'What can I do for you?' he said, trying to sound seductive. It had been a long time, and although Danny was nothing but a cheap prostitute, Paul suddenly thought that wasn't such a bad thing.

''Sallright,' said Danny, who had gone straight to the safe in Eileen's desk and was flipping the combination lock with practised fingers. 'Just got to pick up a few things.'

'You seem to know your way around…' Paul could think only of the things those thick, brown fingers had done to him in days gone by. A safe door wasn't the only thing Danny knew how to open.

'Yeah.' Danny didn't even look up; he seemed, if anything, discomfited by Paul's presence. He rooted around in the safe, found a thick envelope and pocketed it. The door slammed shut, and Danny spun the locks.

'Right.'

'Right.' Was that it, thought Paul? Was that how it ended? A furtive visit – possibly a robbery, he couldn't be sure – and a grunted word of farewell? Not if he had anything to do with it.

'How have you been, Danny? You've been…away.'

Danny wouldn't look him in the eye; it seemed for a moment as if he might be ashamed of his abandonment. 'Yeah. Workin' abroad.'

'So Eileen said. Never seemed to be too sure what you were doing "abroad".'

'Bits and pieces.'

'Oh, I see. Bits and pieces. How nice for you.'

'Gotta go.'

'Wait.' Paul stood in the doorway, blocking Danny's exit. 'You can't go like this. Didn't you at least want…a coffee?'

'Nah, mate, never touch the stuff.' Danny smiled – it was like the sun breaking through the grey March sky, like a Mediterranean summer suddenly bursting into a late Essex winter – and Paul believed that things might go well after all. But instead of grasping him in a passionate clinch, Danny stood up, rearranged his packet (he always had to do this after crouching) and walked towards the French doors. Damn, thought Paul. There are too many entrances and exits in this house.

He followed Danny on to the patio, quite prepared to make a fool of himself if only he could drag his quarry back to the pool changing rooms and rekindle the spark. Perhaps Paul's head wasn't quite as clear as he thought it was, because he tried, for a moment, to look seductive. Men with thinning reddish-blond hair, pale skin blotched from months of drink, thick glasses, bloodshot eyes and incipient paunches are better advised to rely on wit, charm and money to get their wicked way. Paul, however, draped himself over a poolside recliner, crooked one leg and ran a hand through his locks.

'Fancy a drink?'

'Bit early for me, mate.'

'Or a smoke?'

'Nah. Tryin' to give it up.' This was going nowhere, but at least Danny had stopped in his tracks.

'Anything else you fancy?'

Danny took a couple of paces towards the recliner.

At this point the music and the crotches should have swollen, and the action begun. But this was not a porn movie.

Danny laughed.

'Fuckin' 'ell, Paolo, you've put on a bit of weight, ain't ya?'

Danny prodded Paul's gut with his foot. Paul sat up abruptly, brushed the dirt from his sweater and tried not to cry.

'You weren't always like this, Danny.'

'Yeah, well, things have changed.'

'I haven't.'

'Oh, Paolo,' said Danny, leaning down and ruffling the sparse sandy hair like he used to in the old days, 'get a fucking grip.'

He left by the side gate, whistling through his teeth.

Paul tried hard to sober up. He locked the drinks cupboard, engineered a blazing row with Acolola in which he threatened to shop her to the police for 'possession with intent to supply', and started going to a gym in Harlow for boxercise classes. He put himself into the hands of a personal trainer who seemed to know more about Eileen Weathers's private life than Paul did himself.

He forced himself to go into town, see old friends and think about a future outside his marriage. He started writing again, planning novels and screenplays, sending his CV to agents.

He even saw Eileen once in a while. Usually, she was out of the house long before he surfaced; now, he made a point of rising before her and being fully dressed when she (and sometimes Damian) came down to breakfast.

The breakfast table became a war zone.

'Have you spoken to the head of independent commissioning yet?'

'I've left a message, darlin'…'

'He hasn't called me.'

'Look, I have a job to do. Lines to learn. Damian, darlin', pass me the butter.'

'It's all right,' said Paul, deftly beating the tired-looking stud-muffin to the butter dish. 'I'll do that for my wife, thank you very much.'

He slammed the dish down so hard that the lid broke.

'Thank you for that, my darlin'.'

'So when's this contract for research coming through?'

'God, who rattled your cage, Paul? I don't know. Talk to the people at ITV.'

'I have. They didn't seem to know anything about it.'

'Don't worry, darlin'. You'll get the money.'

'It's not the money I'm worried about, Eileen,' said Paul. 'I need a job. I can't sit here all day polishing your Baftas.'

'Ooh, what's the matter, dear?' said Eileen, mimicking Paul's voice. 'Time of the month?'

'This can't go on. I'm a writer. A writer writes.'

'Yeah, well you never seemed to do too much of that before I met you, darlin'. One novel. What was it called? *Frozen Yoghurt*?'

'*The Frozen Heart*, as you'd know if you'd read it.'

'I'm sure it's a lovely book, darlin',' said Eileen, swigging her coffee and preparing to leave. 'The readers at the Beeb said as much, didn't they?'

'Yeah, and that's another thing. Why haven't they…?'

'Good Lord, is that the time? Come on, lover boy, we'd better get to work. Can't sit around here making small talk all day, Paul. Some of us have jobs to do.'

'I'm your husband, for Christ's sake!'

Eileen allowed Damian to help her into her coat and left Paul to finish his breakfast alone.

And so Paul did the only thing he knew how to do: he wrote.

He wrote down everything, all the rumours, the inconsistencies, the suspicions and the downright lies. He remembered it all, from the first day Toby Ross had called him to 'tweak' Eileen's autobiography, through those halcyon days of their first collaboration, his bittersweet affair with Danny, the fire, the trial, the Bafta triumph and the strange coda that had followed. What he hadn't witnessed, he imagined. It poured out of him, word after poisonous word, and he felt elated, relieved, as if he had just been fucked. Which, he realised on reading the manuscript back to himself, he had been. Royally.

He called an agent who he knew would be interested in his story; not the most prestigious agent, and certainly not one who would lead him to

Booker glory, but one who had frequently offered him embarrassing sums of money for just such a betrayal.

The agent agreed to read a couple of sample chapters, so Paul knocked together 10,000 words of vitriol and e-mailed them off.

'And then there are the persistent rumours about Eileen's real gender,' began one particularly promising passage. 'As I have never been granted access to the holy of holies, I cannot comment from first-hand experience on the state of my wife's genitalia, although I know plenty who can, some of them household names. Suffice to say, however, that Eileen's own account of how those rumours began changes from day to day. It was a joke, she'll say if she's in a good mood. It was a lie to hide a deeper tragedy – that's the story for her darker days. There was an abortion, or possibly an adoption, a lost child stolen from her by her husband, or her agent, or her manager, or her mother – always someone else's fault, never hers. All of this somehow explains the story that Eileen was once a boy, a drag queen working in the bars and clubs of London and Paris under the name Kiki de Londres. A desperate transsexual who earned enough money through prostitution to pay for a clandestine trip to Casablanca in the early '70s, whence she returned a "woman"...'

This time Paul didn't have to wait for his calls to be returned. Ten thousand words of matrimonial spite were enough to spark what the agent described as 'a bidding war'. The phone never stopped ringing. The number of journalists staking out the Essex mansion – there were always a few – suddenly swelled, and that was before a contract had been signed or a word published. Paul's online pals learned that he was about to 'go public' with 'the truth' about his marriage to Eileen Weathers, and that he would 'blow the lid off her world of lies and deception'. Paul was playing a dangerous game – and he felt exhilarated. The power of the word, the written word, would triumph over the satanic legions of broadcast.

Paul was getting used to being doorstepped, followed and photographed. He carried on with his 'normal' life, going to the gym, visiting friends in London, fully expecting everyone he met to be somehow on the take. His personal trainer suddenly seemed very inquisitive, as did his old friends; he treated them all as if they were in the pay of the papers, and kept shtum. He took the precaution of lodging copies of his memoirs in a bank vault.

The agent accepted an offer of a £50,000 advance on royalties, with very generous arrangements regarding serial rights, from a publisher with excellent connections with the larger supermarket chains.

Paul moved out of the Essex mansion and back into the Waterloo flat, where he changed the locks and installed bars on the windows.

He awoke one night to hear someone moving around inside the flat. Still half-dreaming, he had a comfortable sense of déjà vu – remembering the last time, when Danny had flown to his side to 'comfort' him – and then suddenly realised that this was not a dream, this was real, and there was someone in the next room.

He leaped out of bed, rushed to the door and turned on the light.

And there, sitting in the armchair with a glass of whisky in one hand, for all the world as if he owned the place, was Danny himself.

'Hello, Paul.'

'How did you…?'

'Got a key.'

'But I've changed the locks.'

'Yeah. The locksmith's an old mate.'

A chill ran down Paul's spine, and he realised that he was wearing only a T-shirt and boxers.

'I'll just get my dressing gown.'

Danny kicked the door shut before Paul could leave the room. The bang resonated in the silence. Somewhere in the distance a police siren squealed.

'You'll be all right,' said Danny. 'Have a drink. That'll warm you up.' He tipped half a pint of whisky into a glass.

'No, thanks. It's a bit early for me.'

'Come on, Paolo. You like a drink.'

Danny stood and advanced towards Paul with the brimming glass in one hand.

'I'm trying to give it up.'

'Shame to waste it,' said Danny. 'Nice single malt. Bet that cost a bob or two.'

'It was a…'

'Still, you're doing all right for yourself, I hear. Drink it.'

'I don't want…'

'Fuckin' drink it.'

Paul realised he was in trouble. He took a sip.

'Don't peck at it like a fuckin' lady. Drink the fuckin' drink.'

Danny was working himself up into a fury.

'But like you said, it's a nice single malt. One doesn't guzzle a single malt.'

'One doesn't guzzle a single malt,' said Danny in a posh, squeaky voice. 'Do I have to pour it down your throat?'

Paul knew that Danny was quite capable of doing just that, and so he gulped down half the contents of the glass. It burned his throat, and his eyes watered.

'And the rest,' said Danny in a calmer voice.

'Give me a chance…'

'Down it goes.' There was a look in Danny's eye that prompted caution. Paul finished the whisky, felt sick and sat down. Danny topped up his glass.

'What do you want, Danny? I don't suppose you've come round for a chat about old times.'

'That's where you're wrong. We need to talk.'

'Well, I didn't think you'd come round to make mad, passionate love to me.' The whisky was kicking in, and Paul felt reckless.

'That comes later.'

They looked at each other over the tops of their full glasses. 'Cheers,' said Danny. Paul, who never could resist another drink, took a swig. He could handle it, he thought; all those months on the Chivas Regal had been useful training.

'I suppose my so-called wife sent you.'

'Eileen's not a very happy old lady just now, Paul.'

'Oh, I don't know. She's got everything she wants, hasn't she? She's got the house, she's got a career, she's got her lovely young boyfriend, she's got more money than she knows what to do with…'

'There's one thing money can't buy, Paul. One thing the old girl values very highly.'

'And what's that, pray tell?'

'Loyalty.'

The word hung in the air like a smell. Paul was suddenly aware of the brightness of the hundred-watt bulb above his head. He stood up to turn it down. Danny pushed him back into his chair, slopping his whisky. It soaked into his T-shirt and shorts like alcoholic piss.

'I just wanted to…'

'Sit down and shut up. You've been a very fuckin' silly queen, Paul.'

'I don't know what you mean. I've done nothing.'

'Christ, look at yourself. You're a mess.'

The whisky was cold against Paul's stomach and crotch, but he dared not move. 'So she knows, then.'

'Yeah, she knows. And she ain't happy.'

'Well, what did she expect? Leaving me alone all day long, preventing me from working. I was going mad in that house. And where were you?'

'I've been busy.'

'You could have called me. You could have come to see me. I thought we were…'

Danny laughed. 'What? Boyfriends?' He said it with a special nasal lisp.

'You led me to believe…'

'OK, Paul. I like you, and so I'm going to tell you a few things that you need to know. Are you sitting comfortably?'

'Well, I'd like to change my…'

'Good. Then I shall begin. First of all, don't kid yourself that you were ever more than a job to me.'

'What?'

'You heard. A job.'

'A bloody good job, then.'

'Yeah, not bad as they go. I've had worse. I've had better.'

'What do you mean?'

'We needed you on our side. You lot are so easy to manipulate.' He made a little pantomime with his fingers; it looked as if he was breaking a chicken's neck. 'You were easier than most. All it took was a pair of shorts and a dirty old T-shirt and you were dribbling all over me, you dirty sod.'

'That's not true. If anything, you were coming on to me.'

'Oh, yeah, sure. I was crazy about you, Paul. Couldn't fuckin' resist. I mean, look at you. You're pretty fuckin' hot stuff.'

Even with all that whisky swimming around his head, Paul realised that this wasn't sincerely meant.

'But that night…The champagne…Dom Pérignon. And then afterwards, in the poolhouse…'

'You never could hold your drink, could you? One sniff of the fuckin' cork and you were putty in my hands.'

'You seduced me.'

Danny threw his head back and laughed. Paul wanted to bite the thick exposed column of his throat, to draw blood from the artery. 'Oh, fuck, that's a good one. Seduced you? Oh, whatever, man. I'll have to remember that.'

'So what are you telling me?' said Paul, slurring slightly. 'It was all a joke?'

'A job. I told you, didn't I? She didn't want you snooping around.'

'So why did she invite me to the party? She didn't have to.'

'Oh, she did. Get you to the party, make you feel special, like one of the family, one of the staff, one of the pets. She's good at that. A few crumbs from the mistress's table, gets 'em every time.'

'Is that how she got you?'

Danny ignored the question. 'But we knew you were a nosy parker, so it was my job to keep you busy while she conducted…business.'

'That's not true.'

'It was so easy. A bottle of fizz, a snog and a fumble and you were out like a light. Then you bloody woke up at just the wrong time, because that silly tart screamed, so I had to make sure that you were out of sight, out of mind.'

'Gemma…'

'That's right, Paul. Have another drink.' Paul hadn't even noticed that he'd emptied his glass and that Danny had topped it up. It no longer burned;

it no longer tasted of much. The air in the room stank of scotch. 'Gemma. She was a bloody nuisance, that girl. Always there when she wasn't wanted. Always making a song and dance about it. She had to be dealt with…'

'You're frightening me.'

'And Eileen's good at that. Really good at that. Thought we'd got her where we wanted her, keeping her quiet with old Lover Boy Livesey. But, no. Silly tart shot her mouth off around town, told tales out of school. That's a stupid thing to do, Paul. A very stupid thing.'

'You mean you…?'

'Killed her? I'll come to that. First of all we had to deal with you.'

'I don't understand.'

'Get you working for us rather than against us. She knew she had to write a book. All part of the master plan. But there was a problem: she couldn't string a fuckin' sentence together, and they were going to take the money back and cancel the contract. So we needed someone to do the job for us. Wash all her dirty linen in public. And so we found you.'

'But why me?'

'Needed someone we could control, didn't we? She spun some story to the publisher about how she'd feel more comfortable with a gay man, did they have any poofs on their books, and there you were, just like that.'

'But why did you have to…I mean, we made love.'

'I don't deny you were a good fuck, Paul. Christ, you were mental for it. Hadn't been getting enough, had you?'

'So it was all planned?'

'And you didn't have a clue. All that business with Jimmy and Gemma, him driving off pissed into the night, Gemma falling down the stairs. But it didn't work out, did it? He didn't crash the car, and she had a soft landing in a bunch of fuckin' lilies. Oh, well, plan B.'

'What do you mean, plan B?'

'He was becoming too much of a liability. Threatening to write his own book, go public with a pack of lies. We don't like people who tell lies behind our backs, do we? Very nasty business.'

Paul remembered the manuscript he had lodged in a bank vault, the bidding war, his stupid fantasies about spilling the beans on talk shows and book tours.

'Yes. I see.'

'Careless talk costs lives, Paul.'

'Right.'

It took a while for these words to sink in to the whisky quagmire.

Paul suddenly whimpered and tried to get up, get out, raise the alarm. Danny pushed him back into his chair; his bottom felt cold as it made contact with the wet cushion.

'So you killed them.'

'Me?' Danny laughed. 'God, Paul, what must you think of me? I ain't a killer.' He grinned, and looked just like one. 'But I know a man who is.'

'He wouldn't be Maltese by any chance, would he?'

'You catch on quick. Better have another drink. Don't want you remembering any of this. Go on. Swallow.'

Paul obeyed.

'You didn't notice a thing, did you? All them phone calls she was makin', all those dodgy blokes coming round the house. You were in a little dream world, wasn't you?'

'I was in love.' Paul could barely form his words now.

'Yeah, and you bought me some very nice presents. See? I still got the chain.' He rattled the gold ID bracelet around his tanned wrist.

'Gold always suited you, Danny.' Paul wanted to cry.

'And any time you started to stick your nose in, all I had to do was walk past the window with me shirt off, and you were as good as gold, writing away like the little classroom swot. It was a piece of cake.'

'Turkish delight...' said Paul through thick, numb lips.

Danny paid no attention.

'But finally I had to make sure you were out the way. The big day. Went so smoothly. The perfect crime. Got you back to the flat, got a bottle of wine inside you, and just in case that didn't do the job, I spiked it with a few of her sleeping pills. Tired you out that afternoon, didn't I? You never did have much stamina, Paul. Left you sleeping like a baby.'

'You were sleeping too.'

'You were snoring before I'd even come, lover boy. Nipped back to the house, just in time for their arrival in the back of a big black car we'd hired specially for the occasion. Didn't know what was going on, poor little fuckers. Thought Eileen had got a big surprise for them, like a divorce settlement or something. They were excited. Then we got down to business in Jimmy's playroom.'

'The webcam…'

'Yeah. Nice touch, that. Gavin's idea. He's a clever bugger. Cleverer than her. Film the whole thing, make it look like a sex game gone wrong. Drag some nutter out of the woodwork, some fat fan who's so fucked up on prescription drugs she doesn't know which way is up, do anything you tell her. She worships Eileen, that woman. Must be mad, fat cow.'

'So it wasn't…Jimmy and her?'

'Jimmy? Nah, he'd never met her before in his life. I set it all up, the webcam and everything.' Danny sounded proud of his achievement. 'Then we put the frighteners on them. Told them they were going to make a little film. Made them do stuff. It was a fuckin' laugh.'

'But why did they go along with it?'

'Oh, that was the good bit, Paolo. Gav's idea, again. Told them it was just to get grounds for divorce. Evidence of whatsit – infidelity. Yeah, get it all on camera, no contest, bang, divorce, clean break, nice big settlement on Livesey, goodbye. They had no idea what was coming.'

'You killed them.'

'Nah, mate. Tragic accident. She dropped a candle, didn't she? Saw that for yourself. Funny the way the fire spread. And him tied up like that, couldn't get away.'

'But she could have raised the alarm.' Paul was having difficulty keeping awake, and dipped in and out of a nightmare.

'Oh, poor girl hit her head. Out like a light. She always was clumsy, falling down stairs and that.'

'So they burned to death.'

'Tragedy. Like the papers said.'

'And you came running back to the flat…'

'Just in the nick of time. Had a shower, got rid of the smell of petrol, fuckin' 'orrible stuff when it gets on your clothes, and you woke up, Sleeping Beauty. And then the terrible news broke.'

Paul was mumbling and sweating. Something wasn't right.

'Chocolate…'

'What?'

'Chocolate and Biscuit. The dogs.'

'Awwwwwww. The doggies.'

'Tell me that was an accident.'

'Paolo,' said Danny with that horrible wolfish grin, 'if it makes you feel better, it was an accident.'

'And then where did you go? I couldn't find you.'

'Had to tidy things up before the cops arrived on the scene, didn't I? Make sure there weren't any evidence that could cause misunderstandings.'

'The bodies…'

'Yeah, had to make them look their best, what was left of them. No nasty cuts or bruises.'

'But the fire spread so fast. It was so dangerous.'

'Well, we thought we might as well make a thorough job of it while we were at it. She was sick of that décor scheme, know what I mean? Kill two birds with one stone. Or three, in this case.'

'I don't understand.'

'You know, Paul,' said Danny. 'Splash it on all over.'

'You set fire to the rest of the house?'

'Yeah. Fuckin' loads of money off the insurance. And all them things she lost. Passport, birth certificate, all that. Terrible, innit? All that stuff from her past.'

'Burned.'

'Not as such. But you know, gone. Disappeared. Poof!' He snapped his fingers in Paul's face. 'Wiped out. Erased.'

Paul remembered something Eileen had said to him long ago, in the first days of their collaboration. 'Wouldn't life be easier if you could just wave a wand and make the past disappear?'

'Her birth certificate…'

'Yep. All that's gone.'

'Like something out of a storybook…'

'Whatever, Paolo. You look pale. Have another…'

'No, thank you.' Paul stood up. 'I think you'd better leave.' He felt suddenly sober and realised the depth of iniquity into which Eileen had led him. The lies, the manipulation, the callous exploitation of his trust and talent.

'I ain't going nowhere,' said Danny. 'Don't you want me to stay?'

'I want the truth,' said Paul.

'The truth?' Danny laughed. 'OK. How do you want it?'

'Straight.'

'Makes a change. Right. The truth. You asked for it. I just hope you don't regret it.'

Danny sat back in his chair, his legs spread a mile apart. 'C'mere,' he said to Paul, who curled up at his feet. He rested his head against Danny's thigh and listened.

chapter sixteen

'She met Gavin Graham back in the early '90s,' said Danny, idly stroking Paul's hair. Now he'd made up his mind to kill him, he could afford to be tender – and Paul was so drunk that he wouldn't remember any of this tomorrow. If there was a tomorrow for Paul.

'She was married to Brian at the time. Now, I liked Brian. He was like a father to me. Lovely man, very solid, dependable, just what I needed at the time. I was running wild, Paolo. Oh, I was a very bad boy. And Brian was the only one who paid any attention. She was always off fucking some boy or other…And then it was Jimmy this, Jimmy that. The papers got hold of it, and so she turned to Gavin Graham. He was just starting out then; he'd been sacked by some big agent and he was touting around the TV companies, picking off any bits of talent that weren't happy with the representation they were getting in house. Well, it was different in them days. Publicists weren't up to speed. Someone like Gavin was bound to come along and drag it all into the twenty-first century.'

Paul had never heard Danny talk like this before. He thought he was a dumb hunk, good at sex and fixing cars but a bit thick in other departments. It was an unwelcome shock. He realised he'd been dribbling into the fabric of Danny's jeans and tried to pull himself together.

'Yeah, Gavin Graham, fucking bastard. He got rid of Brian, handled the whole Jimmy story, got her through the divorce without a hitch and then negotiated a two-year sabbatical from the show; nobody else had ever got that before.'

Sabbatical? Since when had Danny known words like sabbatical?

'Then he got her back in on a better contract: more money, more freedom. Sent Jimmy off to LA with a flea in his ear, made sure he couldn't work, fucked up his career good and proper. I didn't care. I'd fucked off by that time anyway. Couldn't stand being around them two.'

'Eileen and Jimmy?'

'Nah! Eileen and Gavin. Always pawing each other, they were, even when I was there. Disgusting. And poor old Brian, poor old fucker, went without a whimper. I lost a lot of respect for him. I went off travelling…Yeah, well, it was a bad time, Paul. Bad things happened.'

'So you'd known her for a long time…'

'And when I came back, it was all planned out. They'd get her out of *New Town*. They'd get a book done, max the publicity, leave in a blaze of glory, and get rid of Jimmy just like they'd got rid of Brian. But Jimmy, as you know, wasn't such an easy stain to shift. Took a bit more…effort. Still, we got rid of him in the end.'

'It was all planned.'

'Not what you'd call planned, Paolo. Not the finer detail. Sort of made that up as we went along. But when Jimmy started taking the piss with that little tart, it all fell into place, didn't it? She done the crime, she done the time, and when everyone was good and ready along comes Danny with the webcam footage. Ooh, I say, judge, look what's just landed in my inbox! I don't know what it is but I think it might be important. Nice job, eh? I could be an actor, couldn't I? Or a director. That film was a little masterpiece.'

'A snuff movie.'

'And the rest is history. Out she comes, the wronged wife, banged up for a crime she never committed. Wins her Bafta. Book comes out, loads of money. Fucking Six Books? Don't make me laugh. We took 'em for a ride. They didn't have the guts, did they? You gotta have guts in this business.'

Danny's hand dug into Paul's neck. 'And then they gave her all that fuckin' dosh to go back into *New Town*, and they pulled the plug. We hadn't counted on that, but it worked a treat, didn't it? Look at her now! New job, new boyfriend. Oh, yeah, she's still Gavin's old lady, but he doesn't mind. He has his fun too, believe me. I should know.'

Paul's head was spinning, and he wanted to be sick.

'And best of all, she's rewritten the past. She's escaped from all those rumours that pissed her off so much. She destroyed the evidence, she silenced the wagging tongues. Yeah, that trip to Malta was a busy time.'

'What? I thought we were…'

'On holiday? Well, we had a nice time, didn't we, Paul? I enjoyed that. Fucking you twice a day, bombing around on my bike, going off to settle a few scores. Sex gives me energy. Not like you, mate. You fucking nod off when it's over. I want to get out there and…'

'Kill?'

'Yeeeaah.'

'Oh, my God.' Paul retched, and his mouth was flooded with foul-tasting bile.

'Oh, baby, I thought you'd like it like that. You queers like crooks, don't you? The smoking pistol and all that.' He thrust his crotch upwards. 'Well, there's a few tongues that won't wag no more.'

'So the people who knew about her past…'

'Who's to say? There's no one left. Nobody who knew her back then. Oh, the family, they won't talk. Made sure of that. And one or two silly buggers that wouldn't take a warning…Well, we Maltese shoot first, ask questions later. Know what I mean?'

'So you've frightened her family into silence and killed her friends.'

'Frightened? That bunch of cockney cunts? Christ, Paul, they're only interested in one thing. Money. Uncle Keith and Aunt Rose, they'd say black was white for a couple of grand. You should meet them, mate. They're your in-laws. Oh, they're a nice pair. He's done time and she's a smackhead. Easy to manage.'

'And what about the others?'

'Think what you like.'

'Did you kill many?'

'Dozens.'

'You're lying.'

'You should know better than to say things like that, Paul. I might feel like making another movie. Know what I mean?'

'So she really is a trannie after all, then. Kiki de Londres.'

'Tell you what, Paul, I'm feeling fuckin' horny. Any chance of a gobble?'

'No…'

'It's all right. I'm not going to kill you.'

'Yes, you are.'

'Well, then, you'll die happy.'

'I don't want…to die…'

'You should have thought of that before you started telling all them lies in your nasty little book, then.'

'But they're not lies, as it turns out. Why can't she just live with the truth?'

'The truth? You know nothing about the truth, baby.' He started running his hands through Paul's hair, pulling his head closer to his groin. 'You want to know the truth about Eileen Weathers? Your missus? Eh? Well, you be nice to Danny, and he might just tell you.'

Power excited Danny; that much was abundantly obvious as he pushed Paul's face into his crotch. Paul could hardly breathe; the little air he managed to snatch was richly scented.

He did as he was told.

Danny let out a long sigh. 'That's better…'

'So you were saying…'

'Oi! Don't you know it's rude to talk with your mouth full? That's your trouble, Paul. Talk, talk, talk. Don't know when to keep it shut. Big mistake. Aaaaaah…That's better…That's better…' He was caressing Paul's head and neck as if he really cared for him.

'Eileen Weathers. Yeah, funny woman. Well, you should know, Paul. Not exactly the domestic type, is she? Never around when you want her. Doesn't have your tea on the table, eh? You're telling me. Fucking useless in that department. More like a bloke.'

'Mmmmff.'

'Always running around after younger fellers, right? Well, I can tell you a thing or two about that.'

Paul stopped what he was doing for a moment; he felt that the thing he had always feared was about to be made crystal clear.

'Why do you think she always kept me around? I mean, it's not like I had a contract or nothing.'

'Nnnnggggh.'

'You said it, Paolo. Yeah. Fuckin' old bitch. Fuckin' dirty cock-starved old freak.'

This was worse, much worse, than Paul had feared. All the time that he and Danny had been lovers – God, how foolish that word sounded now, in the ghastly buzzing of his whisky-addled brain! – and he'd been giving it to Eileen in her artificial, made-in-Casablanca pussy.

'You didn't know that, did you? That would have made a good chapter for your book, you fucking cunt.' Talking dirty was having an invigorating effect on Danny. He was starting to concentrate less on murder and more on rape.

'Dirty rotten old slag…Aaah…And I was only a kid. A fuckin' kid, Paolo… Jesus!'

Paul slowed down; he didn't want this to be over too soon. The concentration was sobering him up fast.

'What a way to grow up, with that going on all around you. Christ, what a life for a child.'

A child? Paul knew she liked them young – but just how young had Danny been when she first got her hands on him? He was on the point of asking, but it seemed more important to get a bit of air into his lungs. Then Danny said something that nearly stopped him in his tracks.

'Calls herself a mother? Motherfucker, more like…Mother…Christ.'

The word 'mother' was one that Paul never cared to hear in a sexual context, but here it seemed particularly jarring.

'She was never there. Left me behind, soon as she was well enough to leave the hospital, came back to London and picked up her career as if I'd never come along. So I grew up in Malta, didn't I, running around the ports and boats like a native. Didn't speak English until I was six. Didn't know who my mother was…Then they came and fetched me. Might have – unnngh! – left me there in peace.'

Paul nearly choked, and his eyes streamed with tears.

'But that old bitch of a mother of hers, my so-called Nana, she came and took me away, brought me to London. Couldn't have me growing up like a little nigger, she said. I was a Londoner, and I had to grow up among my own people. So I lived in a council flat that stank of piss, with that old drunk setting the place on fire with her fags twice a week. Eventually I got taken into care…Oh, yeah, that's it, fucking yeah…'

It was all falling into place. The mystery trip to Malta, the 'abortion', the reason why she could never have children again – had it been a difficult birth? Danny had mentioned the hospital – the trail of lies and half-truths to cover the one undeniable, shameful truth of Eileen's life: an unwanted, unloved child.

'And then when I couldn't stand it any more, I ran away. Came and found her. I was sixteen. She was married to that old git Charlie Weathers. Had a fuckin' pile of money. Thought I deserved a bit of that. Well, she was all darlin' this and darlin' that, like she couldn't be more pleased to see me. She chucked money at me, got me a car and that, said I could always stay with her, it was my home…All the stuff you want to hear when you're a kid. Got me a few jobs, running errands, and soon I was mixed up with all her dodgy Soho mates. Delivery boy. That's all I've ever been to her.'

Danny was sinking into despond, which was bad news for Paul. He resumed his work with greater enthusiasm, and soon Danny was drifting off into obscenities again.

'Tried to get away, didn't I…? Didn't want to fuckin' land up in prison. Sick of all those old bastards in Soho wanting a bit of my arse…They were all after it, Paolo, and they were willing to pay for it and they loved it, yeah…'

He seemed to be getting too excited now, so Paul moderated his pace once again.

'And then there was the drugs, the coke, selling it, taking it, gettin' fuckin' hooked on it, not that she cared, as long as I kept dealin' it to those bastards out at Bromley. Christ, they got through the stuff. No wonder they kept increasing the number of episodes they put out every week…Oh, God, Oh, Christ…'

Paul was suffocating. He had to breathe. He moved off and concentrated his efforts elsewhere; fortunately, Danny was too far gone to notice. All that practice they'd had over the last year meant that, when it mattered, Paul knew how to make Danny happy. And if Danny was happy, thought Paul, he might have a chance to escape.

'I nearly went down for that…That's it, lick 'em, baby…But I was too smart, and I knew too much about her, so she couldn't just sell me down the river when the heat was on. So Gavin Graham got us out of hot water again, hushed it all up, paid off the journalist that got the story with another exclusive about some politician who raped a callgirl, and after that it was plain sailing. Mummy couldn't do without me. Kept me close by her. And then you came along, Paul, and nearly fucked the whole thing up.'

Then Paul made a mistake. He spoke.

'I didn't mean to.'

This seemed to wake Danny from his reverie, and he realised that Paul was no longer 'silenced' in the way that suited him. He got angry.

'You stupid little bastard. Poking your nose in where it's not wanted. You queers are all the same. How was I ever going to have a life of my own when every time I tried to break away she was always throwing me into the arms of another uncle, another fuckin' colleague who needed a date for the evening, and then you, of all people, you! Some skinny college kid who was so scared of sex he nearly pissed his pants the first time I looked at him.' Danny stood up, his eyes blazing. Paul wished he'd carried on in silence. But instead, he stood up and faced Danny. Paul was a little taller and, although he was dressed only in a wet T-shirt and boxers, he had the advantage over Danny, whose pants were round his ankles.

'I stood up for you when it mattered, Danny.'

'Don't make me laugh.'

'I could have spoken out when the police interviewed me.'

'You knew nothing.'

'I knew plenty.' Paul's head was clear. 'I heard the rumours. I could have told them about all those times when I didn't know where you were – when, I assume, you were busy destroying evidence and covering your tracks. But I chose not to.'

'Yeah,' leered Danny, thrusting his hips, 'because I kept you happy.'

'I see that now,' said Paul, taking a step backwards, wondering if he could push Danny to the floor and run out of the flat.' But I didn't say a word, whatever the reason. I was in love with you, perhaps. I was certainly in love with this.' He grabbed the thing he was referring to, and did something that usually reduced Danny to a moaning wreck. It worked surprisingly well under the rather tense circumstances. 'So I was a good boy, Danny. I did as I was told. I didn't grass you up, did I?'

'You…oh, fuck…It's her…She's a bitch…'

'She certainly is. She may be a bad mother, but she's a fucking awful wife.'

Danny laughed, his eyes closed. He was breathing hard.

'She ain't my mother.'

Paul was getting confused. He couldn't bear another twist in the tale.

'Not no more. She's made sure of that. Covered it all up. Wouldn't do to have a son knocking around, would it? Especially one older than her latest boyfriend. He's a pretty little bastard, isn't he, Paul? Bet you wouldn't mind having a go…'

'So the birth certificate that you burned?'

'Mine.'

'Not hers.'

'Nah, mate…She's cagey about her age, but not that cagey. She's got nothing to hide. Not like she was…unngh!…born a…mmmmfff…bloke or nothin'…oh, fuck.'

Danny's knees buckled, his throat flushed red and he screwed up his eyes. Just at the point of no return, Paul bunched his free hand into a fist, pulled back from the elbow and, with every ounce of force and aggression that he'd learned in boxercise, delivered an upper cut to Danny's solar plexus.

He was out of the door and into Waterloo Road, his wet shirt and pants clinging, before Danny had picked himself up off the floor.

coda

I ran across Waterloo Road. The streets were wet, reflecting the neon signs of the shops and the cinema. At that time in the morning – it was just after three, by Big Ben – there wasn't much traffic. I knew that Danny would be after me, and so I ducked down into the stinking subterranean corridors that lead to the South Bank. Down there I could lose myself, and, more important, lose him.

I charged through the labyrinth and then, when I guessed that he had not followed me, selected my exit, half expecting his hulking silhouette to be blocking my escape. But the way was free, and I was on Waterloo Bridge, looking back down towards what was once – but could never be again – my home. I saw Danny way over the other side of the roundabout, his fists bunched, looking around him like a mad bull, taunted and ready to kill. But he had lost me.

I couldn't think of anywhere to go – there were no friends I could trust – and so I ran, barefoot and clad only in wet underwear, across the bridge and into town. I'd never needed to find a police station before in my life, and had no idea where they were, but I had a dim recollection that there had once been Bow Street Runners, and so I headed up that way. There was no blue light, no comforting figures of bobbies in helmets, just a few drunks and office cleaners. What did I have to do to get arrested in this town?

By now my feet were bleeding, and I was simultaneously sweating and shivering – partly because of my exertions, partly because it was a cold night and I was wet and underdressed, but also, I think, because of alcohol poisoning. I saw a sleeping bag lying across a doorway, and was seized by a desire to crawl in and join whatever was under there.

But I kept on running, regardless of the pain and the blood that was making every footfall stick to the pavement. Finally, on Long Acre, I saw a squad car. I threw myself in front of it: I heard the brakes screech, and I passed out.

I am sitting in a cell in Charing Cross Police Station, where I have been taken for my own safety. I have told my story – about how an intruder in my flat tried to kill me and confessed to the murder of Jimmy Livesey and Gemma Leeds. I have explained that my wife, Eileen Weathers, who married me to silence me and to conceal her affair with Damian Davies, has been party to a series of slayings across Europe. When they smelled the whisky on my breath, the officers laughed and gave me some clean dry clothes (a rather unpleasant, but comfortable, tracksuit, redolent of young police officer) and locked me away 'until you sober up, sir'. They gave me coffee and water and a sandwich, and, when I asked for a paper and pen, were very accommodating. I have written letters to my bank and my agent instructing them to publish the book 'whatever may befall me', and to pay any money it earns to my mother. The police have been kind enough to assure me that they will get the first post.

They have released me with a caution not to drink so much. I dare not go home. I am now sitting in an internet café in Brewer Street. I have written two concluding chapters to my story, relating my married life with Eileen, my late-night visit from Danny and my escape from what I am sure was meant to be my murder. I have e-mailed them to my agent.

I must go somewhere, but I don't know where; they'll be looking for me at my mother's and my sister's. I have no money to pay for the coffee I am drinking. I will have to do a runner.

I hope the book I have written will see the light of day.

I have just seen Gavin Graham on the street. I must fly.